I hope you enjoy this

MURDER MOST UNFAIR

by
Robert Bottomley

In memory of brother Don
and his career in law enforcement

Thanks to
Mary A. Floerke
For editing help

Copyright © 2020
By Robert Bottomley
All rights reserved.

ISBN- 9798621899066

Chapter One

Jenna Botlin stepped lively out of her front door on Culver Street looking up at the bright sun on this gorgeous thirteenth day of April, 2020, in this tourist town of High Point, Wisconsin. Dressed in her gray running shorts with the lavender top, wearing her comfortable running shoes, she was ready to tackle the day with an invigorating five mile run. Moments later, running through the local park, she said "hello" to Joe and Carrie Milam, friends from high school that she still saw occasionally. They too seemed to be enjoying their more casual run as they waved their greeting. Her pace increased as she stepped it up to a measured workout to start her special day.

A short time later, sweating profusely, she ran past Jerry's Pastry Shop, almost tasting and smelling what should encourage anyone else to stop and enjoy. Knowing this was not the time, she pressed on. Her mind began to wander, thinking of past friends and family who had so enriched her life. Smiling at a passing stranger, with these past thoughts still there, she became more alert, realizing her run was coming to a gratifying end, as she once again saw her house in the distance.

Slipping the key in the lock, she felt a twinge of hunger now, as she eagerly showered and changed into work clothes. She was scheduled to work only four hours today, as friends were awaiting her visit later in the afternoon, at Joe's Bar and Grill on Court Street. She cut up an apple into small pieces, scrambled an egg, poured herself a glass of milk and sat down to a slow pace of enjoying her breakfast while scanning some recent mail. Finishing this, she started to envision her day at the help desk at the local library. Aside from the joy of being of help to people, she liked the library environment with plenty of people in a peaceful, quiet state doing what they did. The days passed quickly as there were always more projects to work on to make the library an even better place.

Moments later she was out the door so fast that she could not remember if she had locked the door. She felt safe in her environment as each day was much the same as the last one. The Heiden Library was just a few blocks away, and she enjoyed her walk to work each day. She decided to leave her 2005 Chevy Impala in the garage to save on gas. Her supervisor, Helen Hagen, greeted her shortly after arriving, "How are you doing on your birthday?"

"I'm enjoying every minute of it."

Helen replied, "That is the way it should be. Any directions for your day are at the help desk. Continue to have a good one."

Jenna started working without any difficulties all the way until her shift ended. She walked to Joe's Bar and Grill with a minute to spare in meeting her friends Rae Strong and Jim Hardy at 5:30 p.m. She had known them for five years now and looked forward to the honest discussions and fun. As she opened the door, everyone yelled, "Happy Birthday, Jenna."

Unexpectedly, she froze in the doorway. This had never happened before. Her many friends started pulling her through the doorway, laughing all the way to the room in back set aside for the gathering.

"What's going on?" was all she could think of saying.

Rae responded first, "It's your birthday. We thought it should be a memorable one, so here we are."

"Should I be saying anything?"

"No. We have it from here. Just sit down and let's eat," said Jim.

Before them appears grilled shrimp, corn, hamburgers and other tasty items, with drinks, of course. After this was a time where each friend there told a brief story of a special time in their relationship and offered a gift. What made it unique was the nature of the stories. Some were funny, some uncomfortable and awkward, and others rambling as if not well thought out. Rae started, "I first met you at a party where I was serving drinks, when you were telling a childhood story to someone, when you suddenly stood up throwing your arms in the air saying, that's all. The drinks I was carrying flew in every direction. You were so embarrassed that I could not yell, but instead walked over and gave you a hug."

"Don't remind me. I was so embarrassed." Jenna turned a bright red.

After the first story, everyone was anxious to tell their story. Ed Carpenter, a friend Jenna came to know when she worked at the library a few years earlier, started quietly. "I was minding my own business in the library stacks, with this girl I know, just whispering sweet nothings in her ear." Suddenly Jenna comes up behind me and says, "None of that is allowed in this library." I just walked out of the library without a word.

Jenna laughed and said, "I thought I heard serious words, with the girl looking as white as a sheet. After Ed left, the girl just quietly sneaked away. I regret ever saying anything."

As the night went on with more drinking and the stories becoming more awkward for Jenna, her discomfort began to show. Rae, recognizing what was happening to her, asked. "Jenna, would you like me to drive you home now as you look rather tired?"

"If you don't mind, I would appreciate the ride." replied a person whose day had gotten long.

Rae drove Jenna to her home and walked her to the door where Jenna, not thinking about getting out her keys, just tried to open the door and found it was unlocked. She then realized she had not locked it when she left earlier. Rae realizing what had happened said, "I think I should walk through the house with you to make sure no one is here waiting for you."

Jenna, tired and not thinking clearly, said, "I am sure I will be fine, but if you feel better, come with me to look for yourself." A few minutes later, Rae left, thinking all was well. She did not notice if Jenna had locked the door then.

Chapter Two

Helen Hagen, working at the library the next morning, making her routine look around the library to make sure this April 14th day got off to a good start, was pleased with what she saw as a normal day. An hour later, as she delivered some papers to the help desk, she realized Jenna was not at her station. Lora, usually busy putting books back on the shelves, was at the help desk.

"Lora, why are you working the desk?" asked Helen.

"Without anyone here, I thought I had better stay here until Jenna arrives."

"Jenna did not say she would be late this morning. Did she say anything to anyone else?" asked Helen.

"No one I was around today said anything about it. Do you think it is necessary to phone her and ask if something came up?"

Helen, taking charge now, said, "I will make the call, so I know how to plan our day." Moments later she dialed the number and had to leave Jenna a message to call back when she received this message. Helen then returned to her regular duties while she waited.

At lunch time Helen decided to drive to Jenna's house to follow up and see if Jenna was ill or had another good reason to not be at work. When she arrived and rang the doorbell, there was no answer. She walked around back to see if Jenna might be working there, finding no one. She looked in some windows not covered by blinds but saw nothing unusual. She found no doors unlocked. Thinking Jenna must have been called away unexpectedly, she left to return to work, hoping tomorrow would find Jenna back at work.

The next day, April 15th, when Jenna still had not reported to work, Helen decided to call the police. She started by saying, "This is Helen Hagen at the public library. I am concerned about one of my employees not reporting to work since Monday. I had no luck with a phone message or even visiting her home and am quite concerned about her wellbeing. Is it possible you could go to her home?"

"It has not been that long since you last saw her, but I understand your concern and will have someone stop there today and check with neighbors who may have seen her," responded the friendly officer in charge.

Officer John Smith was assigned the duty to go to Jenna's neighborhood to find out more about where she might be. He, too, found no activity at the home and decided to go door to door asking if anyone had seen Jenna recently. The house to the left of her home was the first stop. A Mrs. Jane Fellows opened the door asking, "Officer, is there a problem in the neighborhood?"

"Jenna Botlin hasn't shown up for work the last couple days. Have you seen her recently?"

"I don't believe I have since three days ago. You may want to ask Mrs. Cramer, the house on the other side of Jenna's," Mrs. Fellows replied.

"I will do that now. If you should see her, please call the police department."

The officer then rang Mrs. Cramer's door, only to find no one home, so he decided to go across the street and knock on a door. Joe Smith, a retired man, opened the door, greeting the officer, "What can I do for you today, officer? I noticed you going door to door."

"I am inquiring about the whereabouts of Jenna Botlin. Have you seen her lately?"

"I saw her three days ago about seven in the morning as she started her five mile run. She looked just fine then. Has something happened?" asked Joe.

"We don't know. Her employer has not seen her at work since Monday. Apparently, it is not like her to just not show up," said officer Smith.

"You are right about that. She does not miss work. She doesn't even miss her runs in the morning, a responsible one, that one."

Officer Smith asked him to call if he should see her. After talking with other neighbors with no new information, he called in to his superior to ask what he should do next. Apparently, none of the neighbors had been given a key to Jenna's house. He was instructed to go to the library and talk to Helen, and possibly others, who might have a key or know of relatives or friends who did.

Chapter Three

Arriving at the library, he found Helen, asking, "Could we talk somewhere private where I can ask you more about how to contact people who might have a key to Jenna's home?"

"Follow me to my office, please."

Helen began by going to her files to look for contact people Jenna had given her when she was hired. Listed was a brother by the name of Jim Botlin and a phone number which she gave to Officer Smith. She knew of no one who might have a key. Next she provided him names of fellow workers who related well with Jenna: Cheryl Frye, Ben Cummlo, Carol Jenkins, and Todd Geskgell.

"Thanks for the information. I will speak to these people in person soon. Which of them knew Jenna best? Do you mind if I speak with that person here today?" asked Officer Smith.

"I don't mind at all. My concern is for Jenna's wellbeing," remarked Helen.

Since Todd Geskgell was the name he was given, Officer Smith approached him at the library and asked, "I am trying to locate Jenna Botlin and was wondering if you could answer some questions for me now, or if not now, set a time to meet?"

Todd, who was somewhat uncomfortable with a policeman approaching him at work, replied, "I don't feel comfortable talking here. Could we meet somewhere else after work?"

"Would you give me your address and phone number and give me a time that works for you?" asked Officer Smith.

Todd completed the request, setting a time for seven that evening. The officer then went back to the police station where he called Jenna's brother Jim on Jim's cell. With no answer, he left a message for him to call the police department in High Point and ask for Officer Smith. He thought to himself how unusual it was in this community for a person owning a home not to have a backup key left with a neighbor or friend. Was there something in Jenna's background that she was afraid of someone finding out about? She seemed rather young to be paranoid unless she had a bad experience earlier in her life. If Jenna was not found soon, he would have to pursue those thoughts. Suddenly, he was startled as the phone rang bringing him out of his reverie. "Hello, this is Jim Botlin calling back."

"I am glad you responded so quickly," replied the officer.

"It is with concern I called, since I am not used to getting calls from the police. I hope nothing has happened to my sister Jenna."

"I understand your concern. I don't know if anything happened to her. Her employer was concerned when she had not shown up today or yesterday. She is not home, and I was wondering if you know where she might be?" asked the officer.

"I have not heard from her for a couple of weeks and have no knowledge of her planning to be away from work or High Point."

"The neighbors I have met don't have a key to her house. Do you have a key to check and see if she is ill in her home?" he asked.

"I do and only live an hour or so from you. I can meet you in about an hour, as now I am starting to worry," said a now concerned Jim.

"If you can do that, I will be waiting for you there," replied Officer Smith.

Jim quickly announced, "I will see you then." The phone went dead.

Officer Smith now went to his superior to fill him in on what was happening. His superior was Police Chief Harry Mathews, in charge here for the last ten years. Both men quizzed each other about who might know her whereabouts. They had to be ready for more serious possibilities, now; however, they both thought getting into the house and finding no signs of foul play would ease their concerns. In an hour or so they should know more.

At one in the afternoon Jim Botlin pulled into his sister's driveway, seeing a police car parked in front of the house. He quickly got out of his Buick and walked quickly to meet Officer Smith. After introductions both men walked to the door where Jim opened it, and both men went to the living room.

Once in the room the officer asked, "Do you mind if I go first since there was no response to our asking if anyone was in the house?"

The house was a one level ranch with a basement. Each room looked in order until they got to the bedroom. Officer Smith ordered, "Please stop here while I examine the room more closely." He had noticed what appeared to be blood on the bed near a pillow. He pulled out his Glock from its holster and opened the closet finding no one there. He now, using gloves, slowly stepped toward the bed and slowly pulled back the covers, seeing blood on the sheet.

He rushed to the other room where he asked, "Jim, no one is in the house. Let's leave the house so I can call my superior."

Jim just stood there, as if not hearing the officer, pale and tired looking. He looked at the officer's face searching for answers, fearing the worst, then walked quietly outside.

Officer Smith, once outside, asked Jim if he would mind waiting in his car. Jim did just that and sat staring into space.

Trying hard not to show alarm, Officer Smith called Police Chief Mathews, "I am at Jenna Botlin's house now, with her brother sitting in his car in shock. I had just come out of Jenna's bedroom where I saw blood on a pillow. I put my gloves on and lifted the covers seeing blood on the sheet."

Chief Mathews took charge saying, "Stay there until someone else can relieve you. I will call the forensic team in Madison to see how quickly they can get here. Ask the brother to pull his car over to the other side of the street while you wait. Then have him sit with you in the squad car and try to calm him down, maybe by having him talk about his sister and what she has been doing since moving here."

After following those instructions, the two men sat and waited. The officer started the conversation by saying, "Jenna is not in the house, and I don't know where she is. I did see what I believed might be some blood and cautiously called to have someone more expert than myself come and look at it."

"Do you think someone killed her?" inquired Jim, fearing the worst.

"All I can tell you is that we have been trying to locate her since her boss became concerned since she had not showed up at work, which was unlike her without calling in. We have only heard good things about her from coworkers and neighbors. She has no enemies that we know of. Finding something out of the ordinary has now prompted our action."

"I'm glad I came today and hope this leads to finding her and helping her," stated Jim, putting on a brave face.

"We can only hope for the best, while sharing some of what she has been doing since moving here."

"She moved from Chicago to find a safer place to live and work, and to get away from a bad relationship with Jerry Lensor. They had been dating for about a year."

"What happened to end it?" inquired the officer.

"Jerry had been getting more possessive and demanding of Jenna. She realized this was not what she wanted in a relationship and told Jerry that. He just would not accept it and stalked her for weeks, so she decided it was time to leave," was Jim's grateful response. "She purchased a 2005 Chevy light gray Impala to drive to Wisconsin."

"Did he have any knowledge of where she had gone to?"

"If he did, it had to have been following her out of Chicago through his stalking. She had been careful and saw no sign of him upon her leaving," Jim said, confident she had succeeded.

"It sounds like she made a good decision as there is not much future with such a controlling person in her life," reflected a concerned officer.

"You don't think he found her do you?" asked Jim, showing more concern.

"I will try to relieve you of that thought by doing a check on where he might be these days, if that is fine with you."

"I would like that," said Jim, as a period of silence came over them until they both saw another police car pull up behind them.

Both men got out of the car to meet the arrival of Chief Mathews. After a brief introduction the chief asked, "Could we keep your key until a copy can be made?"

"Yes, here it is. I will do whatever I can to help you find my sister."

"Could you stay in our town for a few days while we sort this out?" asked the chief.

"I have a room at the local Best Bed and Breakfast at 249 North Westfield Drive, just a few blocks away. You have my phone number. I will wait for your call, as you may have more questions," replied a most cooperative Jim, anxious to find his sister.

"Thanks for your help today. It might be better if you are not here as we go through the house looking for information leading to your sister. Get some rest until we get back with you," said a grateful chief.

"Will you be able to come to the station tomorrow some time to continue this discussion? It could be helpful in solving whatever problem we have here," said the chief.

"I can see you will be busy here for the day. I will see you tomorrow at two in the afternoon."

Jim drove off in his car, just as the forensic people arrived from Madison. While they went to work, Officer Smith spent time wondering what Jim might have to offer tomorrow. Maybe Jenna just had an accident and maybe she went to a friend for help with her injury.

When forensics left, he had just enough time to make that appointment with Todd Geskgell. He arrived at his place at 723 Dodge Street, about five minutes early, just before seven. It was dark this time of year in April. He was surprised to see no lights on in the house. He decided to wait for five minutes or so to give Todd time to get there. After ten minutes he was not surprised to find no answer. He called the station to let the officer on duty know where he was.

Tired of waiting, he walked around the house to see if any doors might be open, and also used his flashlight to see if he could see in the windows. That was getting nowhere until he got to the kitchen window. Shining the light toward the floor near the sink, he saw a body. The clothes looked like the clothes Todd Geskgell had been wearing that morning. He called the station for backup and an ambulance. Within ten minutes they were there breaking down the door to find the dead body of Todd. Again forensics was called in. The first report indicated he was hit on the back of the head with a heavy object, definitely not an accident. Maybe there was merit to Todd's being uncomfortable this morning at the library. What was he afraid of then? If it was the police, it implied some earlier crime. If not the police, then it must have been someone afraid enough of what Todd might say to kill him before talking. What is the secret he knows about, and does it have anything to do with Jenna Botlin?

Chapter Four

The next morning, April 16th, Sheriff Rex Hardy was talking to Police Chief Harry Mathews when Officer Smith walked in. Last night's murder created a sense of emergency for law enforcement. He asked if he should still keep his appointment with Jim Botlin at two in the afternoon. Both men agreed that it was time to find a motive for this crime and the possible disappearance of Jenna Botlin. It was beginning to look like a connection.

Computer work was needed to do a search on the backgrounds of these two people. Officer Smith was asked to get the names and addresses of everyone at Joe's Bar and Grill on April 13th at the time of the birthday party. Then they would do a criminal check to try to narrow down the list of suspects. The next thing on everyone's mind was the forensic evidence from both houses.

Sheriff Hardy planned to inquire about people moving into the area recently who might have a criminal record. The three would meet soon and share information. Chief Mathews would follow up with forensics and also meet with Jim in the afternoon, giving Officer Smith more time to follow up on those in the bar.

Officer Smith first looked up where Rae Strong might be today. He found her at work behind the counter at the local post office. Since it was not that busy at the time he arrived, Rae got someone to work as customers came for her. They found a place out back to talk. Each pulled up a folding chair nearby. Rae spoke first, "I imagine this is about Todd or Jenna."

"Yes, it is. Just to follow protocol, can you tell me where you were yesterday afternoon and evening?" inquired Officer Smith.

"I suppose it is your job to eliminate suspects at this point. As you might be able to guess, I was at the post office working until five. Jim Hardy met me at The Old Fashioned Diner at 5:30 p.m. where we ate fried cod with a salad and roll and talked about our day. From there we went to the local theatre at the 7:00 p.m. show. We watched a movie called "1917", a very good movie by the way about World War I."

"Thank you for that information. Next I would like a complete list of all at Joe's Bar and Grill the night of Jenna's birthday party," requested the officer.

"Ed Carpenter was there. From the library staff there was Chery Frye, Ben Cummlo, Carol Jenkins, and Jerry Hadley with his date Terri Anderson, both in a bowling league with Jenna, and Ken Jones, a person Jenna ran with from time to time. If I think of others, I will let you know as they come to mind," stated Rae with almost no hesitation. She seemed like a person that did not miss much, was what was going through the officer's mind before he spoke again.

"Was there anything out of the ordinary said or going on that night as you look back on it?"

"The story about Jenna finding Ed Carpenter in the library with a girl was something I had never heard before that night. Jenna blushing after hearing it seemed rather odd. It made me wonder if there was more to the story. What else might have happened?" said Rae as she silently looked down, as if trying to recall if anything else was said.

"Did anyone else say anything about it?"

"No. It actually got kind of quiet for a while before others started sharing stories," said a somewhat puzzled Rae.

"I heard about your story. Tell me about others that night."

"Most were personal in nature and not memorable. Ben Cummlo told about the first time he saw Jenna. She had just stepped out of a dark blue colored car with a group of beautiful yellow roses in her hand into the rain. She turned around with what appeared to be a frown and almost ran from the car before going into Jerry's Pastry Shop."

"What was the point of the story?" asked a puzzled Officer Smith.

"That is just it. It was never made clear by anyone there. People just moved on to hear the next story. No one thought anymore of it," reported Rae closing the chapter on that tale.

"Were there more stories that night?"

"I am sure there were, but that is all I can recall at the moment," said Rae as she looked back to work stations, implying she should be getting back to work now.

"Thank you. Please get back to me if you recall more of what happened that night." Both got up and put the chairs back where they found them, with Rae briskly walking back to work, and the officer slowly walking out of the post office, taking in what he just heard.

Officer Smith decided to stop for lunch at Joe's Bar and Grill to listen to people talking about recent events while he ate at an out of the way booth, where he would be less noticeable. He ordered a cheeseburger and a chocolate malt, while he watched who was there and what was being said. He was half way through his burger when he heard a lady at the bar say to the bartender, "Has business been affected by the recent events in town?"

The bartender, used to this question by now, replied casually, "not much. Most of the same people keep coming back. Newcomers stop in to see what might be happening in our town, gossiping about it somewhere else."

"What do some of your regulars think happened to these two people?" asked the curious lady, as if it were an everyday question.

"Everyone has their own theory about that. Some think Jenna just got roughed up by someone and decided to leave town. Some think Todd Geskgell ran with some bad people and had no way out from whatever he was into. Most are just trying to figure it all out in a way that does not reflect badly on the community."

"I see what you mean. Hopefully, law enforcement will figure it all out in time so the rest of us can sleep better at night," summed up the lady, ready to move on to other topics.

With no other discussions revealing, Officer Smith walked over to the bartender and asked, "Who was the lady asking you the questions a few minutes ago?"

"I knew you were near us and thought you might talk to me. She is Jessie Cornwall who moved here about six months ago and operates The Dress Shop on the next block. She doesn't come in that often. Most of the time she is asking about certain people and wanting to know their names, probably since she is new in town. She tends to be a name dropper to use in a way to draw people into her shop."

"Had she previously asked about Jenna or Todd?" quizzed an inquisitive Officer Smith.

"She may have. I just don't remember."

"If you remember more or hear about fairly new people in town, stop and see me," said the officer as he left, satisfied the whole thing was probably just some wanting to keep up with local gossip.

Officer Smith now returned to the police department to fill in his chief and find out more before further follow up. Driving up he noticed Sheriff Hardy's vehicle already there. Not wasting any time he walked in and saw him meeting with Chief Mathews in his office. With the door closed, he lightly tapped on the door and waited before entering.

Both men acknowledged him and asked him to sit down and inform them on his findings so far today. He told about Ben and Ed's comments the night of the birthday party, and gave them the names of people present from Rae, and a brief comment about Jessie Cornwall's questions at the bar.

Sheriff Hardy asked, "Who is Jessie Cornwall? I don't think I have had the privilege of meeting her before. Is she new in town?"

"Six months or so. She runs The Dress Shop on the next block from the bar, asks a lot about who people are and wants to know what is happening in town," replied Officer Smith.

Captain Mathews chipped in, "I met her at her business a couple weeks ago when I was shopping with my wife. She was helpful and pleasant at the time."

Then he got down to business. "Forensics has informed us that the blood was Jenna's on the sheets. It was enough to suggest a fairly serious injury such as a blow to the head or a knife injury. She wasn't in the bed long enough to suggest dying there. It appears she was moved fairly soon after the incident. It is not known yet whether she was forcefully removed or just helped in order to move her to a location to help or contain the incident."

Sheriff Hardy then added, "No one else's blood could be found. Whoever took her was careful not to leave a trace of what may have happened there."

Chief Mathews announced, "We plan to inform the press of our findings, suggesting she may have been injured and taken from the house, and we are asking citizens to inform us if they have seen her in the last three days. Of course, we ask them to be alert in notifying us if they should see her in the near future. We will also look for where her Impala may be."

Sheriff Hardy now reported on the murder of Todd Geskgell. "Yes, forensics confirms it is a homicide with a blunt instrument being used. We are waiting for more information from them about the scene. The press knows about the killing but not much information. I have released Todd's name and pertinent information about finding the body since family has been notified. Again, the press will be asking the community to provide information someone may have and report it to the police or sheriff's department."

Chapter Five

April 17th started with Sheriff Hardy in bed, ready to get up and start his day, when his thoughts turned to Jenna's brother Jim. He knew Jim was staying at his good friend Felicity's Best Bed and Breakfast nearby at 249 North Westfield Drive, and now decided to start his day with a quick visit to see Felicity and update her on events and ask her to listen to what people are saying in town, as she knew most everything happening before he did. At the same time he might get a chance to meet Jim there to get more history on Jenna and any connection to Todd Geskgell. He felt strongly that the link between these people would lead to future arrests down the road.

After showering and fixing a quick breakfast of an egg and toast with a hot cup of tea, he felt even stronger about making the visit right away this morning. Moments later he was saying hello to his good friend, "Felicity, how are you this fine morning? May I come in for a short visit?"

With a hug and brief kiss on Rex's cheek, she smiled saying, "You are always welcome here. It's early. Would you like some breakfast first?"

"I just had something before coming."

"Let's go sit where we can be comfortable then, since I know your brief meetings can take a while, probably job related," replied Felicity in a more serious tone now.

"I have two items in mind. The first is I know you have pretty good tabs on what is happening in our town. Since you know something about Jenna and Todd, I would like to have you listen to what you are hearing about the two of them and keep me posted. I understand Jim, Jenna's brother, is staying here for awhile. Have you had any conversations with him yet?"

"I will do what I can to help you. I have had some conversing with Jim as he is so worried about his sister, and with the murder he is afraid his sister's absence will not get the attention it deserves," chipped in her brief comments.

"What exactly does that mean? He isn't foolishly going after suspects he has in mind, I hope."

"For starters he does not understand why no one has found Jenna's 2005 Impala. He plans to look for it himself and make inquiries," informed Felicity in a matter of fact way.

"Is Jim here now? I would like to talk with him," asked Rex even more concerned now about the direction things were going. He knew it was time to intervene before something else happened.

"I will check now and be right back," said Felicity as she hurriedly walked away. Five minutes later she returned with Jim introducing him. "Sheriff Hardy, this is Jim Botlin. Jim said he would like to talk with you now." With that said, she quietly walked out of the room, leaving the two men to talk.

"May I share my concerns now?" replied a concerned brother.

"Let's sit at the table here, and I will try to answer your questions and add a few of my own," said the sheriff as he prepared for a lengthy session.

"Why have I not been informed about what you have found out to this point?"

"Mostly it is because there has been little learned about your sister, her car, or her work friends or her past experiences. That is the biggest reason I am here today," was the direct answer given by Sheriff Hardy.

"I'm sure the murder of Todd Geskgell has taken more of your time too," said Jim showing he did understand some delay.

"First of all, do you have any idea where Jenna's car might be?"

"That is what I planned to do today, search for myself and make calls to people here and past people who have known her and her friends," announced Jim, proud to do what he could for his sister.

"Be careful. Anything suspicious I want you to call me. Here is my card. I will continue looking. If nothing useful is learned in two days, I will report your sister missing and start a wide search with other law enforcement members suspicious of kidnapping," promised the sheriff.

"It's that kind of quick response I have been looking for. I will do as you say hoping it is not a kidnapping. Can I help you in any other way?" said an eager participant who would do anything to find his sister.

"One last thing. Would you make a list of people she has known well, some whom she may have had a reason to dislike, family and friends, workplace encounters, etc.? Get that information to me as soon as you think you have a complete list," said Sheriff Hardy, as he stood up in preparation to leave.

Shaking hands now, Jim empowered by what just took place, announced, "I will do just that."

Sheriff Hardy next drove to the police station to plan the next steps with Police Chief Mathews. He found him at his office on his computer. Giving him time to finish what he was doing, he asked, "Do you have a few minutes?"

After a few minutes Chief Mathews said, "I have more information on Todd Geskgell. It is confirmed he was hit on the back of the head with a blunt object as we suspected. He died sometime between 5:00 p.m.

and 7:00 p.m. the day we found him, only hours after Officer John Smith had talked with him at the library. It means we will have to try to find a connection between Jenna Botlin's disappearance and his death. Several partial fingerprints were found in the room where his body was found. It will be interesting to see whose those might be, other than Todd Geskgell's. Since the doors were locked when we arrived, I wonder why the killer locked the door again upon leaving. Did he have a key to enter or did he just find one to keep people out for as long as possible? There was part of a foot print where the killer may have stepped on blood. That may help narrow down possible suspects we find."

"How much of that do we want to withhold from general information at present?" asked the sheriff.

"We can let it be known it was blunt force trauma to the head. Let's keep the rest to ourselves in narrowing down suspects. Let's send Officer Smith back to the people working at the library, asking about his friends, work people, enemies, relationships and anyone who might have a key to his house," suggested the chief.

The sheriff now mentioned a known fact. "His vehicle was left in the garage, not missing like Jenna's car. Has it been checked for fingerprints?"

"It has and once again they will be checking those against the ones found in the house," replied the chief.

"I noticed that Geskgell's cell phone was left in his pants pocket where we found the body and that Jenna's cell phone has not been found. What do you make of that?" asked Sheriff Hardy.

"It could be the killer did not plan this attack. It may have been rage at something said. If it had been planned, it could mean the killer was not worried about names or information found on the phone," replied Chief Harry Mathews. "Do you have other thoughts?"

"Not right now. I'm just trying to see connections between the two incidents and coming up empty. I just talked with Jim Botlin and told him in two days we would have to declare his sister a possible kidnapping and do a broad search for her 2005 gray Impala. Should we do it sooner?" asked the sheriff in a cooperative spirit.

"I think so, to show we are trying to be thorough in our investigation. Since we now have a murder, we should move it up to this afternoon. Call Jim and let him know so that he doesn't panic more thinking the worst. It is a precaution on our side. Tell him that," replied the chief.

"Let's do a search of electronic records regarding Todd Geskgell's bank records, computer, mail, etc.," commented the sheriff. As both men nodded approval to what had been discussed, they separated to start work with Sheriff Hardy stepping out to inform Jim of the change in plan.

After the call to Jim, Sheriff Hardy reminded himself to follow up on the whereabouts of Jerry Lensor to see if he was still in the Chicago area or closer to our town.

Chapter Six

April 18th found Jim driving the streets of High Point, looking for his sister's car without any luck. He then went back to Best Bed and Breakfast to start his list of names for the sheriff. He went back many years to come up with a long list. He started by calling all the relatives he could to inquire about any possible friction between them or other relatives and Jenna. Without finishing the list, he decided to take a break and ask Felicity if she had any food he could pay for, as he was hungry and did not feel like driving to a restaurant.

He found her talking to someone on the phone. He patiently waited and found her to be agreeable to providing him lunch. As if this were a normal event in her life, Felicity said, "Sure. I am happy to make lunch. Just give me a few minutes. Do you want to talk while I make it for you?"

"If you don't mind, it might help me clear my head, as I have been calling so many relatives to inquire about any past or present conflicts Jenna may have had. I have had no luck thus far. Jenna kind of kept things to herself, so I am not surprised coming up with nothing so far. It isn't that she didn't have problems. She just tended to keep them to herself, as she sometimes tended to trust the wrong people. She was naive that way," rambled on Jim, not fully realizing the possibilities in what he had just said.

"Since you knew her so well, that means you have to read between the lines and guess from what you know who some of those not so nice people might be. Start your list after lunch on that note to see if it helps," suggested Felicity.

After eating a hot ham and cheese sandwich with pieces of an apple and some potato chips washed down with a glass of chocolate milk, Jim felt recharged to make that list before making more calls. He thanked Felicity and went to his room to work.

As he walked toward his room, Felicity shouted, "If you think any of the conflicts could be serious in any way, come back and talk to me before making the call please. Be careful who you stir up."
Officer John Smith returned to the library to finish his interviews, this time including information on Todd

Geskgell. He walked up to Cheryl Frye saying, "I'm Officer Smith here today investigating the death of Todd and the disappearance of Jenna. Can I take a few minutes of your time?"

"I have been expecting you since you called on others already. What can I do for you?"

"First, let's clear your alibi for the day Todd died and the days Jenna did not show up for work," said the officer.

"The afternoon Todd died I was working here until 5:00 p.m. Then I drove home and had supper and watched television for the evening," said Cheryl.

"Was anyone with you after 5:00 p.m.?"

"Just me and my cat," reported Cheryl.

"Where were you after the party for Jenna and the following day?"

"I was not invited to the party. I went to a movie called 'The Joker' at the theatre downtown by myself, then came home about 10:00 p.m. The following day I worked here," said Cheryl.

"Next tell about times you have seen Todd and Jenna together."

"I saw them together at a movie in January, the movie about Mr. Rogers starring Tom Hanks. I saw them another time at a restaurant one night in February," said Cheryl in a matter of fact way.

"Have you ever seen them disagreeing about anything, and can you give me a name of anyone else who may have seen them together?" asked Officer Smith.

"They were having a good time when I saw them. Ben Cummlo told me he saw them in a car together once. That's all I know."

"Thank you for your help. Can you direct me to where Ben Cummlo works today?" asked Officer Smith with a smile.

"He works just around the corner at the book checkout desk."

Officer Smith walked up to Ben casually and said, "I am Officer Smith, investigating the Geskgell murder and the disappearance of Jenna. Do you have a few minutes?"

"Yes. Others can check customers out. Can we move over to a table?" replied Ben.

"Were you at Jenna's party or know others who were there?"

"I was not there, but I think Carol Jenkins, Ed Carpenter, and Joe Milam were there," was the quick response.

"Were any of these people close to Jenna and Todd?" asked Officer Smith.

"I think they all knew each other. I think I saw all of them at Joe's Bar and Grill in February one night drinking. They appeared to be having fun together and sharing stories," said Ben as casually as if talking about the weather.

"Have you ever seen just Jenna and Todd together anywhere?" asked Officer Smith.

"It could be, but I don't recall such a time," he answered with a puzzled look as if trying hard to recall a time.

"Thanks for your help. Have you ever seen them possibly in a car together?"

"It could be. I am not sure. If I recall it, can I give you a call?" asked Ben.

"Please do. The question I have been asking is to confirm where you were the night of Jenna's Party and the next day during the afternoon and evening," stated Officer Smith.

"The evening of the party I drove up to Madison to shop and hit the bars. The afternoon the next day I worked here until 5:00 p.m. and then drove back to Madison to see a friend," he said.

"Can you give me the name of the individual you met, and were you with anyone else?" asked the officer.

"I'd prefer not to give you any names. Some might frown on what I was doing."

"If you change your mind or have more to offer, please call me," was the officer's last statement as he walked away after handing Ben his card. On the way out of the library, he thought to himself what a difference from the last time he was here. Carol, Ed, and Joe Milam would have to be seen soon. It was beginning to look like connections were being made.

Chapter Seven

It was now April 19th. Sheriff Hardy decided to focus on learning more about Jerry Lensor and also finding Jenna's Impala. To speed up the process he put through a call to his friend in Illinois, Sheriff Briggs, who helped him a while back solve a case involving someone in Carpentersville.

"This is Sheriff Alester Briggs. What can I do for you this early April morning?" was the cheerful response to Rex's call.

"This is Sheriff Hardy in High Point, Wisconsin. We worked together not long ago on an arrest that started with information you gave me from Carpentersville, Illinois. I'm hoping you might help me get information on Jerry Lensor."

"I do remember our working together on the Terry Shaw arrest. I would like nothing better than to work with you again. I can't say I know anyone named Jerry Lensor though. Can you give me what information you do have and what he might be involved with, or should I say who he might spend time with," was the cooperative and helpful voice Sheriff Hardy got to know earlier.

"I am working two cases currently that may or may not be connected. The first is of a Jenna Botlin who came here about five years ago from the Chicago area to escape a controlling boyfriend named Jerry Lensor. She picked up a 2005 Chevy Impala and drove here apparently without his knowing. She is well liked here, but disappeared around April 16th. We found blood on her bed a day or two later and have not found her car," summarizing Jenna's situation.

"That information could help me. What is the second case?" inquired Sheriff Briggs.

"Jenna worked at the local library with a young man named Todd Geskgell who we were scheduled to interview about his connection to Jenna. When we turned up at his house for the interview, we found him dead from being hit over the head with a blunt instrument. His car was found in his garage. The relationship between the two was not well known," the sheriff summarized briefly what he knew of the relationship.

"I can see how there might be a connection. Let me see what I can find about both of them and any connection they might have. It appears both parties may have secrets they didn't want out there. Find those secrets and you will be close to an arrest," he noted as one plausible theory of opportunity and motive in the early stages of this investigation.

"My thoughts are similar without facts yet. See what you can find out, and I will continue searching. Let's keep in touch with our findings and hope for more good results like the last time. It feels good to be joining forces again. I will send you license plate information," said a welcoming Sheriff Hardy. The call ended with Sheriff Hardy thinking how far cooperation can go in making life better in our communities.

Ten minutes later Officer John Smith walked into his office. "What is new since the last time I saw you?" asked the sheriff, as soon as he spotted him coming toward him.

"In my interviews at the library, I find that many of these people are connected. Jenna and Todd have been seen together several times. Ben thought Ed, Joe and Carol were at the party. It appears Jenna and Todd were together with these same people at Joe's Bar and Grill in February, drinking and sharing stories, just having a good time," summarized John.

"Who is the Ed person you are talking about?" asked the sheriff.

"His name is Ed Milam. I don't know him. That's why I am here to ask you more about him before I interview him."

"I don't know everyone here. Let me ask here in the office if anyone knows him before checking records," replied Sheriff Hardy.

He walked out of his office and returned a few minutes later with news. "A secretary here knows Joe and Carrie Milam quite well. She went to high school with both of them here in High Point and thought Jenna was there at the same time. Joe manages the local Ace Hardware here, and Carrie works as a waitress at the truck stop. She says they are good people," said the sheriff.

"Have you found any criminal activity involving Jenna and these people here in High Point?" asked John.

"They appear to be good citizens which makes it hard to see local suspects in our investigation thus far. That said, there have to be people here who know more than what they are telling us. No one just disappears without a trace in the size community we have," commented the sheriff, wondering to himself what is secretive that creates such suspense.

"I am going to start by looking up Joe Milam at the hardware store in an effort to uncover some of these secrets," announced John as he walked out of the office.

Shortly after lunch he walked into the Ace Hardware store, asking the clerk at the cash register, "Could you tell me if Joe Milam is here today?"

The young girl looked up with a large smile saying, "I think he is back in row eleven."

Officer Smith walked up to the young man scanning the shelves and asked, "Are you Joe Milam?"

"Yes I am. How can I help you find what you are looking for today?" said Joe, saying what any customer would expect to hear.

"I'm Officer John Smith, inquiring into the murder of Todd Geskgell and the disappearance of Jenna Botlin.

Is there anywhere more private where we can discuss what you know of these two people?"

"Certainly. Let's walk back to my office and sit down," was the cooperative attitude the officer expected to hear.

When both were sitting comfortably, Officer Smith started his questions, "Let's just start with how you might know these two individuals."

"I've known them since our high school days here. We have been together socially from time to time. Since I am married and they are single, we don't have as much reason to get together as say our married friends do," was the frank but friendly response.

"Have you seen either of them recently?"

"The last I saw of Jenna was when my wife and I were taking a casual run a day or so before her disappearance when she ran by us and acknowledged us. I believe it was her birthday that day. She seemed happy as I recall."

"What about Todd Geskgell?" asked the deputy?

"Todd is usually more of a private and quiet person, unless with friends. It has been a while. I think it may have been when many of us were together at Joe's Bar and Grill weeks ago. It was a good place to go and unwind after a busy workweek."

"Who else was at the gathering as you can best recall?" asked Officer Smith.

Taking a moment to recall. He finally said, "Jenna, Carol Jenkins, Todd, and maybe Ben Cummlo were there. I'm not sure since many of us were at Jenna's birthday party also."

"Who do you think was not at both gatherings?" asked the officer.

"I'm not sure Ben was at the birthday party," was his thoughtful response.

"Do you know if either Jenna or Todd had enemies or may have been in a disagreement with anyone recently or even a long time ago?

"Not that I know of. Jenna left High Point after high school to go to Chicago and just returned about five years ago. I am sure it took a while to regain contact again. If that is all, do you mind if I get back to my work?" Joe asked.

"If anything comes to mind, just give me a call at the police station," stated the officer as Joe Milam walked back to aisle eleven. Officer Smith thought Joe Milam was being honest in his response, but was not sure whether he knew more than what he was saying. He wondered if his wife, Carrie, knew either person in a more social way. He made a mental note to himself to come back if more connections were made than just mentioned.

Chapter Eight

April 20th started well at 249 North Westfield Drive at the Best Bed and Breakfast as Jim Botlin had just finished an egg omelet with toast and cherry jam and a hot cup of coffee. He waited until other guests had left so he could talk with Felicity.

Felicity could not help but notice Jim sitting alone yet. She walked up, smiled at Jim, reflecting her pleasant nature, and asked, "What do you have planned for the day?"

"I was hoping you would have a little time this morning to listen to my experience calling relatives and friends about my sister and advise me on what to do next," stated Jim.

"Since no one else is here at the moment, get your notes taken and tell me what is happening. I will help if I can or direct you to people who can help," replied a willing participant and the good neighbor that most everyone knew in High Point.

"My list is in three areas: relatives, work place, and friends over the years. I tried to think of who Jenna might most likely share her hopes, fears, and failures, as all of us have those three things in our lives. The question is who would Jenna share that kind of information with. In the last six years, I have that concern because I have seen Jenna grow more quiet with me. She shared less as time passed when nothing bad had happened between us," stated Jim, pausing to ponder that last thought.

Noticing that pause, Felicity put her hand against her face carefully and said, "It sounds
as if the last six years have not been as kind in some ways as previous years in her life. It could mean something bad happened to her before moving here, that she cannot or will not face if she can help it. Maybe someone showed up in her life again, reminding her of how unsafe life can be again. Who could that person be and what happened to her before getting her life back here?"

"Exactly. It sounds easy. In reality it is hard as people don't want to share what they know," said a frustrated Jim Botlin.

"The problem is, all have secrets they don't want shared. We have to be shown that some people may be in trouble and unable to get out, unless other caring people drop hints of anything they know, that could get that needy person back to a good place again," thoughtfully replied Felicity.

"Easier said than done. They clam up on me or even say they can't get involved in things they know nothing about," said a puzzled Jim.

"Then I suggest you do it softly by saying you are looking for any hint to help your sister. You don't need to know all the details if they don't want to share it. Just ask for a hint of trouble to point the way to helping your sister. Say how much appreciated that would be and that your plan is not to spread that information around, but only to narrow down the search in the quietest of ways. Others don't need to know all the circumstances," said Felicity, in her gentle way of providing help but not forcing the issue.

"Are you telling me I have to start all over again?" said a disgruntled Jim.

"I am not. I will show you. Take one person at a time and tell me what they have said or shared. I will only listen to what they don't want to say or what hint they might be giving you," said Felicity.

"Let's start with our mother. If you sort out all the nice things she says, all I could come up with is this. Jenna has been happy since coming back to High Point. Chicago started well and ended up poorly. Everyone loves Jenna," said Jim.

"It tells me everyone does not love Jenna. Something happened in Chicago that caused her to leave. Have you talked with anyone she knew in Chicago or anyone in her life she shared what happened in Chicago?" inquired Felicity.

"My father did say some guy in Chicago did not treat Jenna well, and Jenna did not want to talk about it, and was shutting up," said Jim.

Felicity said, "It tells me one thing. What made her learn to shut up? She must have been talking to someone, and it ended up hurting her. That means we are talking about more than one person with a secret. We need to know who she talked to. Who would she have shared that with?"

"I do know where she worked in Chicago and one person named Jane who worked with her there. I don't have contact information though," said Jim.

"This is where I tell you who to see to get that information. Call or visit Sheriff Hardy and ask him for help with it. Will you do that before continuing?" asked Felicity.

"Thank you. I will do it today. Thank you for being such a good listener," said a grateful Jim Botlin.

Jim immediately phoned the sheriff's office asking for Sheriff Hardy. He was put through to him. "Hello, what can I do for you, Jim?"

"I have been making calls to relatives to find out more about Jenna and her difficulties. Felicity has been helping me. She suggested I call you to let you know where Jenna worked in Chicago and the name of an employee named Jane, who worked there, whom she shared things with. We thought you might have a way of reaching her to further delve into what may have been wrong. Jane worked at Penney's in downtown Chicago."

"Thank you for the information. Let me think about the best way to go about this. Keep trying to find her friends in case they may know something more to share with us. Just be careful not to put yourself in danger," said Sheriff Hardy.

After thinking about it, he called Sheriff Briggs in Chicago. Sheriff Briggs was surprised to hear from him so soon. "Well, have you solved your cases and don't need my help?"

"Hardly. I'm calling for your advice on how to best handle a situation that just came up. Do you have a few minutes?" asked Sheriff Hardy.

"I do. Fire away."

"Jenna Botlin worked with a lady named Jane at Penney's in downtown Chicago. I am thinking that Jenna knew too much and mentioned it to some of her friends, causing her to leave in a hurry. If I were in Chicago, I would go visit Penney's and look up Jane to interview her in a non-threatening place, to see if she has any names or information to give us direction in solving the disappearance of Jenna. I suspect the last thing she wants is to be involved in any way making a phone call more difficult. What are your thoughts?" asked Sheriff Hardy.

"I agree. It may be difficult even talking to her in person. Are you asking if I would be willing to make this visit?" asked Sheriff Briggs.

"Yes, but I understand if you don't. I will figure it out one way or another," said Sheriff Hardy almost apologetically for making such a call.

After a long pause, Sheriff Briggs responded, "I will see her personally, but I am not sure how soon it will be. If that works for you, I will meet her and get back to you next week."

"I accept and appreciate the offer. If it doesn't happen, get back to me also. I will try to make it up to you. Let's hope it leads to something," explained Sheriff Hardy with relief. Both men said their goodbyes.

The sheriff then called Police Chief Harry Mathews who answered promptly. "What can I do for you, Sheriff?"

"I was wondering if we should meet yet today to bring each other up to speed and make adjustments if needed," said the sheriff.

"Can you be here in the next hour?" Chief Mathews asked.

"I will see you soon."

Forty five minutes later both men were sitting together at the police station. Sheriff Hardy started the update, "Jim called me with Felicity's help to tell me about one of his sister's friends who she worked with in Chicago who might know something about Jenna's experience there. I then called Sheriff Briggs in Chicago and he offered to look up this Jane lady at Penney's in downtown Chicago."

"It might lead to a clue of who we are looking for," said Chief Mathews.

"One other thing. Earlier today I called Sheriff Briggs and told him a possible theory about our two cases with first Jenna's disappearance only to be followed by a murder. The first case involves Jenna leaving Chicago because of a bad situation involving Jerry Lensor. There may or may not be a connection, but I asked for his help finding out more about this Jerry Lensor and he's getting back with me."

"It can't hurt since you two have a good relationship. Anything we get to solve these cases is welcomed," summed up feelings by the chief.

"What do you have going from the police angle?" asked the sheriff.

"You may have heard some of this, but here goes. Officer Smith, at the library again, discovered that Jenna and Todd were seen together on various occasions. Joe Milam, Jenna, Todd, Ben and Carol had socialized at Joe's Bar and Grill together at least once. Most have stated alibi's that we can check out. Ben appears to not want to give an alibi. I don't know if it implies trouble for Jenna or an effort on his part to help her. We may want to watch him for a while," summarized recent developments by Chief Harry Mathews.

"I'll help by having a deputy drive by his place and see where he might be going nights or other off hours. We need to find out what he is caught up in," suggested Sheriff Hardy.

"It shouldn't take too much effort to know," said the chief.

"It is strange that Jenna's car has not been seen by someone," mused the sheriff.

"I am beginning to think we may have to look at other explanations for it," suggested the chief.

"By the way, hopefully Felicity will help Jim make more contacts regarding who Jenna knew and what she knew," suggested the sheriff.

"Has more forensic evidence come in yet?" asked the chief.

"I am not aware of it. Maybe it is time for a call to find out," said the sheriff.

"We might want Officer Smith to ask more people at the birthday party about what stories they have heard lately from that party or others," said the chief.

"We can agree that there are too many secrets that we will find out about by delving deeper. It will make the bad people out there nervous eventually. If they were afraid someone knew too much before, it is our job to make them think it is not over for them," suggested Sheriff Hardy

"That is it for today. Let's give some thought to that last idea in our future efforts," was the last statement made before both men left for the day.

Chapter Nine

April 21st; Southern Wisconsin was beginning to show signs of spring with the days getting longer and more frequent sun and the lifting of spirits among the citizens of High Point. In the early morning after breakfast at the Best Bed and Breakfast, Felicity and

Jim Botlin decided to take a leisurely walk in the neighborhood.

It wasn't long before Jim brought up what was on his mind lately. "I know it is early to learn what happened with the information turned over to Sheriff Hardy, so I made more calls since then. When Jenna first moved to Chicago, she mentioned getting to know a neighbor named Frieda Morsetty on West 71st Street. I searched the net and finally found a phone number that might match up to that street. I placed a call to find out."

"That is good thinking to go back that far to maybe better times for Jenna. Was it the person Jenna knew when you called? Was she reluctant to get involved?" asked Felicity, wanting to learn more about Jim's skill in approaching people.

"I get it. You are worried I might come on too strong and scare them away."

"It did cross my mind. Your response tells me you took time to warm up to Frieda Morsetty and may have learned something. Am I on the right track?" inquired an impatient Felicity.

"Why don't I tell you how the conversation went, and you can decide for yourself. She appeared to recognize the name of Jenna, but was leery about talking since she did not know who I might be. That is when I told her I was Jenna's brother, shared when Jenna moved to the neighborhood, and told a few stories about childhood events back in Wisconsin that would help her see Jenna's personality and interests," said Jim, as he paused, wondering how much more to share.

"I like your approach. Was she still reluctant or did you have to mention that she was now missing?" asked Felicity.

"That is exactly what I had to do for fear she would say she was busy and hang up on me. When she processed what I said, she paused enough to make me think she still might cut the call short. Instead, she showed concern by asking what I wanted from her. I wasted little time as I immediately asked if Jenna had met someone then who might not have been good for her," said a sober looking Jim, before continuing the story.

"I did not care for some of the individuals she befriended and spent less time with her because of them. Since she moved shortly after this, I did not worry about them or her, until your call. If I give you any names, I do not want my name used. Is that understood?" Frieda said.

"That shows me the good side of Frieda with her being brave enough to want to help a person she liked and cared about and yet try to protect herself. I hope you gave her your assurance to reflect a sense of trust to someone who befriended Jenna," suggested Felicity, implying how important it is to be able to trust and show confidence to honest people, which will encourage them to keep such good habits.

"I tried to limit her fears to the extent I was able. She then told me about a young man named Franco Darenko who got a little rough with Jenna at times, and at other times bought her expensive gifts and took her to expensive restaurants to stay on her good side, and use her in some way not made clear to me," explained Jim, trying to capture as much of what Frieda had said, without missing too many little details.

"Were there any hints of what Franco did for a living or where he lived?" inquired Felicity.

"No. That was all she would say about him," said Jim.

"Who else did she mention?" asked Felicity.

"Jack Ramset was who hung out with Franco and did not talk much. It was not clear whether he was a friend or fellow worker. Both men were white men with a bit of a chip on their shoulders according to Frieda. She did not like them and stayed away from them. She had hoped Jenna would respond in the same way," summed up what Jim learned from Frieda as he continued to walk without saying more.

"Do you mind if I pass on this information to my good and trusted friend Sheriff Hardy without mentioning Frieda's last name?" asked Felicity.

"I was hoping you could pass it on in a discreet way. That way I can continue talking to people in Jenna's past in my effort to find her and bring her home," explained Jim now getting emotional as his eyes watered.

"You are doing the best you can for your sister. Be patient as we hope for the best results. Trust what your gut tells you and be patient and rather careful, as sometime soon, we will meet up with people who won't take kindly to your questions. Please back away quickly when that happens and let Sheriff Hardy know immediately, as he will know more about how to handle such people," spoke a most caring Felicity.

"Thank you for listening to me. I am going back to my room now. Have a good day," said Jim as he walked on for a short while.

Upon returning, Felicity made a call to Rex passing on the information with as much detail as possible. He reassured her he would get back to her and Jim when he knew more.

Sheriff Hardy then began his own investigation in any criminal history for Franco Darenko and Jack Ramset. Petty theft was all he could find on Jack Ramset. Franco Darenko on the other hand proved to be a man with a past in crime. Disorderly conduct, theft, beating on women and some men, but with many dropped charges in that area, gang ties, etc. Sheriff Hardy wanted to call Sheriff Briggs right away, but decided to give him time with his first request before bringing up these two names. After all there was not much in the way of criminal behavior yet concerning Jenna. She may have just tried to get away from it all, in order to protect herself and her friends. Sheriff Hardy was beginning to feel more urgency before something bad was about to happen. He didn't have to think about it long as a call came in from Chicago. "Sheriff Hardy speaking."

"This is Sheriff Briggs getting back to you sooner than expected. Jerry Lensor has skipped town. Some of my law enforcement friends know Jerry quite well as a hot head, not known for making rational decisions. The word is out on the streets of Chicago that he believes his girlfriend left him for another man. He has apparently been trying to figure out where she went for a while with no luck. Somehow he heard she originally came from southern Wisconsin. He was on his way to Madison to find her wherever he could, and bring her back to Chicago with him, or possibly kill her if she didn't come."

"That can't be good. Do you have a recent photo of him? I would like to be prepared for him by letting law enforcement in our part of the state know who is coming our way. Do you know what vehicle he is driving and pertinent information about it?" asked an even more concerned Sheriff Hardy.

"I will electronically send you all I have on him now. He is a registered owner of a Colt 45, which is almost expected for the cowboy mentality he has. Don't expect a rational response if you stop his car. It could turn violent in a hurry," offered Sheriff Briggs.

"I appreciate your help. I also have received two other names of people who act much the same way. They made visits to Jenna where she lived when she was first in Chicago, maybe five years ago or more. Franco Darenko and a follower of his named Jack Ramset. Franco appears to be a control freak who likes to throw his weight around. I don't know what their connection might be to any of this otherwise. If you want to follow it, fine. If not, I will pursue it," suggested Sheriff Hardy.

"I will inquire as soon as I get a chance. Let me know what happens to Jerry Lensor. I think my city will be better off without him," bluntly stated Sheriff Briggs.

"I'll get back to you soon. Thanks for the help," responded the sheriff, hanging up now to get the information coming in and let other law enforcement people know.

As soon as he had the information, he let local law enforcement know first, starting with Police Chief Harry Mathews. "Harry, I just sent you electronic information for your people to be on the lookout for this black Chevy Malibu, driven by Jerry Lensor, coming our way to find Jenna, and take her back to Chicago with him, or possibly kill her if she won't go. He is armed and dangerous with a temper management problem. Take necessary caution. I think he is coming from Madison. I will let Madison law enforcement know now. Let me know if you see him coming."

"Will do," responded the chief.

Sheriff Hardy then notified the Dane County Sheriff and also let Grant County Sheriff Jason Reed know, just in case Jerry Lensor came in from the southern direction. He realized how little they had to hold Jerry Lensor on if they captured him. It would not stop him from going after Jenna. If anything, it might make him realize how close he is to finding her. He needed to find her in a hurry, but how? Then he had an idea. If this is the reason Jenna left, then others in High Point were probably helping her and doing a good job so far. What if we send Officer Smith back to the people he interviewed, letting it slip that someone was on his way from Chicago and thought he knew where Jenna was. Out of concern for her safety, would it cause a caring person in the know to come to either Officer Smith or myself?

He called Police Chief Mathews, explained the plan to him, and asked, "What do you think of the plan? Could it work or make it even more dangerous?"

"Let's do it since we are not having much success currently. You might want to inform the brother of what we are about to do. If he hears about it from someone else, it could cause him to lose trust in our operation or put himself in danger," announced the Chief.

"I agree. I will do it in person, now, before putting it into effect," announced the sheriff hurriedly.

He then drove to see Felicity to inform her of the plan. He wanted to do this to reassure himself it was the right course of action and also to get her to go with him when presenting the plan to Jim. Arriving he saw her just walking into the Best Bed and Breakfast. He parked and walked in behind her asking, "Hey pretty lady, what are you up to these days?"

Turning around with a large smile, she said, "Wouldn't you like to know?"

"A guy has to come see his girl once in awhile or he might lose her," was his romantic response.

"Why are you really here? What do you want from me?" she snapped back.

"Is Jim here?"

"I believe he is," she said curiously now.

"Let's go where it is private so I can share my plan with you," he said.

Walking into an adjoining room, she said, "Spill it now, please."

He did just that and then asked, "What do you think of the plan?"

"It could backfire if the wrong people pick up on it. On the other hand, we are not having much success currently. It is worth a try," she said.

"Will you come with me to share the plan with Jim and help calm him down if necessary?" asked the sheriff nicely.

"That's why you are really here, isn't it?" Felicity said pretending to be angry.

"Yes. I need your help because he trusts you, and I need his trust right now."

With that over with, they quietly walked to Jim's room and knocked on the door. He said, "Come in."

They walked in with Felicity saying, "We would like to talk with you briefly."

"No. Has something happened to Jenna? Is she alive?" with fear written all over him.

"That is not why we are here. We still don't know where she is. However, we have heard of someone coming for her from Chicago, someone who wants her back with him. We don't think she would want to go with him," explained the sheriff.

"What is it you want from me? I want you to protect her," said Jim.

Felicity took charge now saying, "We want to protect her, too. Our problem is we do not know where she is to protect. We want to find her before others do."

"What can I do?" asked Jim frantically.

Sheriff Hardy said, "We have a plan, but we didn't want you hearing about it, thinking you were not included. We are wondering if Jenna knew there was someone she knew who might come after her, and she ran away to protect herself. If so, that means she may have used local people she trusts to protect her."

"I had thought that same thing, thinking it must be working, until you brought me this new story. If someone is coming, the situation could get suddenly worse in a hurry. What can we do?" asked Jim.

"We want Officer Smith to go back to those he interviewed and tell them that someone is on their way from Chicago right now to take Jenna back with him, or possibly kill her if she won't go," explained the sheriff.

"If she gets word of this, it might scare her even more, causing her to break away from her hiding place. Then this man might see her before we do," said Jim.

"It is possible, but we think one of her friends may come to us for help now, since she is in a more threatening situation," replied Felicity trying to calm Jim down for fear his sister could be hurt or worse.

"It sounds like it could work. Then I could be with my sister again soon. Is there any one of these friends that you might contact first to see if he would ask for help rather than letting so many know of it?" asked Jim, trying to find a less risky way.

"There is one person without any real alibi that could be contacted that way. If he doesn't go for it, the message would not work with the others," stated the sheriff frankly.

"Is there any way you could hold him in jail for a while if he chooses not to cooperate?" asked Jim.

"Arresting someone without cause is a serious thing. I don't think we could get away with that," said the sheriff.

"What if after interviewing him, and he doesn't want to get involved, I just come into the police station, saying some guy just attacked me a couple hours ago and tried to rob me, but I fought him off?" asked Jim.

"That could cause us to hold him for a day or two."

"Can we try that yet today?" pleaded Jim.

"Let me call the Chief and ask Officer Smith to drive where this person is to see if he would have an alibi for right now. If so, we might be able to."

While waiting for a response from the chief, Sheriff Hardy formulated the timing needed to possibly make this work. The chief finally called saying, "Officer Smith has been in a place not visible to this person and says he would have no alibi for this time. He will stay there until I call him telling him to drive up and bring the person in as a suspect for questioning. When he arrives, I will call you to come to the station where the two of us will question him again and share what we know to get him to admit he knows where Jenna is. If it does not work, I will step out where Jim will be making his allegation of an attack on his person by our suspect an hour or more earlier."

The time came to start as the Chief said, "Officer Smith has confronted Ben and is bringing him into the station for questioning. You can come with Jim to the station now."

When they got to the station, Sheriff Hardy asked, "Jim, will you stay in the car until I come for you?"

"I will."

The Sheriff walked into the station and found the Chief. The Chief said, "Let's both walk in together, and then I will ask the officer to leave while we interrogate the suspect."

Before long the two of them were sitting across from a frightened Ben, saying, "We are not making an arrest at this time. You are just a person of interest right now. Is that clear?" asked Chief Mathews.

"What is it that I supposedly have done?" asked Ben quite surprised.

"You have no alibi, and we suspect you have taken Jenna Botlin against her will," explained the Chief.

"Jenna is a friend. Why would I want to take her anywhere?"

"That is precisely our question. What explanation do you have for being with her?" asked the sheriff.

"Who told you I was ever with her?" asked Ben.

"There are those you work with who always know more than people think."

"I want to know the name of my accuser now," said an angry and frustrated Ben.

"That will come in due time. Own up to your part in Jenna's disappearance, so we can get this over with," said Sheriff Hardy with a firmness in his voice.

"I will never say anything about Jenna, no matter how much you question me," said a stubborn Ben now.

"You care for her that much, do you? If she should refuse your needed attention, would you think about doing away with her?" implied Chief Mathews rather sarcastically.

"You don't understand anything. I'm no threat to Jenna. It is just the opposite," said a frustrated Ben rather honestly thought both men.

"Did you ever think that we are of the same feeling?" asked Chief Mathews as sincerely as he knew how to be.

"Then why are you treating me this way?"

"I'm glad you asked. We need your help now. Law enforcement officials in Chicago have notified us today that a man Jenna knows has heard where she is, and is coming now to get her to take her back to Chicago with him. If she refuses, he plans to kill her. So you tell me why you are here at this very moment," explained Sheriff Hardy, as directly as he knew how to.

"So let me go now so you can get this guy," said an exasperated Ben.

"Once again you fail to understand the urgency here," said Chief Mathews.

"Then what do you want from me?" asked Ben possibly beginning to understand the situation Jenna is in.

"If we find this man, we cannot arrest him, because there is no crime. He is just looking for a girl we can't find either," said Sheriff Hardy.

"That isn't fair. He could kill her in the meantime," announced Jim, who had walked in.

"Now you finally get it," announced the Chief.

"You must think I can tell you where she is in order to protect her. Is that right?" asked Ben.

"You tell us, Ben. The ball is in your court now," said Sheriff Hardy with a sharp tone to his message.

Ben paused for a little while and said no more except, "Can I leave?"

"What do you think?" replied Chief Mathews sarcastically.

"If I knew something, I would tell you because I do care about Jenna," said Ben, in a rather unconvincing way, as far as the two men were concerned who were staring at him intently.

"If you won't help, then you leave us no choice but to announce to everyone listening, that a man is coming from Chicago at any time to take Jenna away forever, alive or dead. Tell us where she is, so we can help her or let her go forever. Without your help, that is what we are left with. If you can live with that, so be it," said Sheriff Hardy, showing his lack of patience.

"All that will do is help him find her, and you know what that means," said Ben.

"It took a long time for that to sink into that fat head of yours, Ben Cummlo. Now what have you decided to do about it? At this point the responsibility for what happens to Jenna is on you, not us. We do not have her to protect. Do you understand?" said Sheriff Hardy, in the harshest of tones once more.

"I do understand. I'm just not sure what is best for Jenna."

"You have reasoned it out by now and know what is best for her. We do not have such a luxury since we do not have Jenna here to protect her and set up a plan to draw in the potential killer for us to arrest. What is the reasonable thing for you to do for all concerned Ben?" asked Chief Mathews.

"O.K. I get it. I have to decide what is best for Jenna," said a bewildered young Ben Cummlo.

"We are waiting on you, Ben. The clock is ticking. What have you decided? Are you going to help or not?" asked Chief Mathews as if he has not asked it enough times already.

A now sweating Ben said, "You are right. I know where she is and will tell you. I want what is best for Jenna and always have."

After a long pause, Ben said, "I will take you there now."

"Thank you, Ben. We all want the same thing. Let's get her and protect her now," said Sheriff Hardy.

As Chief Mathews took Ben to his police car and drove to the place where Jenna was, Sheriff Hardy stayed behind to make sure his people were in place to assure success in this endeavor.

Six miles west of High Point to a farm with dilapidated buildings no longer in use, is where Chief Mathews drove his police vehicle, wondering if this was a ploy or not. He used his radio to confirm his thoughts to a deputy behind him. Ben assured him from the back seat that a door opened in the back that led to a basement where a light was on. Ben asked, "May I go to announce our coming as Jenna is probably scared at this point?"

"I will have my deputy drive up behind us and watch for other exits before you and I go," said Chief Mathews.

That done, both fellows got out of the car and proceeded to the rear of the building slowly, with Chief Mathews now drawing his gun, in case he needed it quickly.

Ben opened a door. Light shown down a stairway. Ben said loudly, "Jenna, this is Ben. I'm coming down."

Ben walked to the basement with the Chief a few steps behind. The Chief heard Jenna say, "Are you sure it is safe?"

Ben assured her, as he turned toward her, "It is safe. I have someone with me you can trust."

Then Jenna saw Chief Mathews behind Ben, "You didn't do this. Now I will be out in the open to be found."

"Actually, Jenna this is for your benefit. We are at a point where you need protection over hiding," said Chief Mathews.

"Who knows where I am?" asked Jenna, looking very frightened now.

"We will explain that when we know you are safe Jenna. Is there anyone else down here?" asked the chief.

"No. Just me."

The Chief used his radio to let everyone know she was safe. "We are bringing her out now. Be prepared to safely put her in the back of your vehicle now," was his command to the deputy.

With Jenna safely in the car, the vehicles proceeded to the police department where she was securely locked up with a deputy staying with her until superiors arrived. Chief Mathews and Sheriff Hardy walked in to see her securely safe in the cell.

Chief Mathews asked Jenna, "Are you hungry for anything in particular?"

She said, "I would like something warm and tasty if possible."

The Chief said, "Would grilled chicken and mashed potatoes with vegetables work for you and a cup of hot coffee?"

"I can't tell you how long it has been since having something like that."

"Are you hurt in any way where you need a doctor to look you over?" asked the chief.

"No. I have been well cared for."

"While we are waiting for the food to be prepared, let's get a woman in here to get you to a shower and cleaned up with fresh clothes. After you have eaten, we will explain what is happening, and why you need protection more than what you have had. Are there any questions before we do that?" asked the Chief in a kind fashion.

"No questions at the moment. I will get settled in for now," said a compliant Jenna.

"Good. I will be back to talk after you get cleaned up and have had something to eat," said the Chief as he walked out to call Sheriff Hardy.

Sheriff Hardy and the Chief had a frank discussion about how to best confront Jenna with her actions and her secrets. Chief Mathews started the conversation, "Let's start with being happy she is safe again, before asking about secrets. Let's be friendly in trying to find out who has been helping her and why."

Sheriff Hardy responded agreeably, "I concur, but at some point, we need to inquire about her past to identify more suspects who may be out to kill her and for whatever reason. I suspect her fear is so strong that she will not give us much to work with."

The Chief replied, "I agree that she will appear to be cooperative, but will not completely trust that we will be able to help her in this fight, or she would have come to us before now."

"Then we have to prove our value to her to win that trust. We will try to get some names from her, protect her, and then finally let her know our plan to capture the person coming for her. The question is, should we confide in her who that person is, if she is not forthcoming to us? If she holds back, should we?" confided Sheriff Hardy.

Both agreed to that strategy before agreeing to meet with her at the jail to start the discussion. On arrival they witnessed a more relaxed Jenna, who could now smile, giving the appearance of looking forward to the upcoming inquiry. "It is good to feel safe again, back where my friends are," stated Jenna, being friendly and looking healthy and composed.

Chief Mathews responded in kind by smiling and showing his good natured side, "I speak for everyone in our community when I say we all welcome you home."

Sheriff Hardy now spoke, "We are here to help you in any way we can and hope you feel the same way."

"I will help you to the extent I am able to do so," was Jenna's carefully worded response, not knowing exactly where this discussion could lead.

"You have lived here for five years happily with lots of friends. What prompted you to suddenly leave us?" asked the chief.

"It was not a choice I wanted to make. I received an anonymous note at my door when I woke up after my birthday party warning me that someone was coming from Chicago to do me harm. Not knowing exactly who that was, I decided quickly to hide until I could figure out what to do next, not knowing how long I would have to hide," reported a frightened looking Jenna.

"Do you still have that note?" asked the sheriff.

"I do not. I burned it in fear of putting this person in danger," replied Jenna.

"Did the handwriting look familiar in any way?" asked Chief Mathews.

"It did not, but the message was clear," sighed Jenna, conceding her fear then and now.

"Am I to understand that you met some undesirable people in your stay in Chicago?" asked Sheriff Hardy.

"I was rather naive when I moved to such a large city. I did not always make good choices in whom I associated with at the time. It appears I am now paying a price for such bad decisions," admitted a repentant Jenna, happy to unload such a burden.

"I will admit all of us make poor decisions at times, especially in our youth. What are the addresses you lived at while you were in Chicago?" asked Chief Mathews.

"At first at 230 West 71st Street and later at 840 South Playmore Drive," answered Jenna without hesitation.

"In which place did you feel safe?" asked Sheriff Hardy.

"Neither. There were some good people in both neighborhoods, but the people I got to know weren't among them. Not knowing many people in Chicago, the men I met at work, and socially, mostly hung out at bars and with friends of like interest. Out of loneliness I went along and got caught up in whatever they were doing and their discussions," Jenna admitted, quite frankly, about her situation at the time.

"From what I do for a living, I understand how easy it is for people just starting out in life and wanting to be liked, to make judgements of others that can come back to hurt them. It takes experience with people to sort out who has our interests at heart and who does not. Life gets better for most of us once we can do that. I'm sure your experience taught you that when you moved here," commented Chief Mathews, sounding a little too preachy he realized as he finished his thoughts.

"Your point is well taken, and I did make adjustments here that made me feel safer and happier until I received the note. My regrets are catching up with me," said a sad young Jenna.

"I just thought of something that might be interesting. What if I just asked you for names you know from any of those social, bar, or dates you had, no matter how good or bad the relationship. It may add up to nothing or set a pattern for us. Would you write some of those down and give those to us now? Others you can write down later," said Sheriff Hardy.

"Since most were short term, I will not have much of a list for you. I will give you names that come to mind at the moment," said Jenna as she wrote out a brief list and handed it to the sheriff.

"Thank you as anything helps us at this point. Give us the others as you have them. Where is your Impala?" asked the sheriff.

"A friend, at my request, is keeping it hidden. I would prefer not to get them in trouble for helping me," said Jenna rather firmly. With a long pause now, she appeared to be firm regarding protecting her friends.

"I'm sure you know that a person you know was murdered the day after you left here," announced Chief Mathews solemnly.

"I am aware of that."

"How can you be sure it is not connected to what is happening to you?" asked the Chief.

"I don't know how it could be connected. He was a good person who did not deserve to be killed by anyone I know of," stated Jenna.

"Did he have feelings for you?" asked the sheriff.

"Do you mean did he love me?" asked Jenna, with a puzzled look on her face.

"Is it possible?" asked Sheriff Hardy.

"Not to my knowledge," said a tired looking Jenna.

"We will conclude this interview for now. Do you have anything you would like to ask us?" asked Chief Mathews.

"How are you going to prevent me from being killed?" asked a worried looking Jenna Botlin.

"We will get back to you with our plan shortly. We could use more help from you if you are willing to provide it. We feel you know more than you are sharing," said Sheriff Hardy.

"If I can think of ways to help you, I will let you know. I'm just too tired to think anymore tonight. I need to sleep and think about everything," stated Jenna, as the men got up to leave for the night.

As the sheriff and chief left for home a short while later, they both agreed to meet early the next morning to work out the plan. Sheriff Hardy had to make one last stop for the night.

Moments later he kept his promise by asking Felicity to go with him to inform Jim of what had happened and where we might go next.

Jim answered his door looking as if he had been asleep. "I didn't know how soon I would hear from you, but I hope it is good news."

Felicity announced with a smile, "Jenna has been found safe and well."

Jim, overwhelmed with happiness, had to sit down on his bed with the weight of all he had on his mind. "I am so grateful. Can I go see her now?"

"We are here to ask you how you can help us when you do see her. She must know you are here, but has not mentioned knowing it. That puzzles me," said Sheriff Hardy.

"I don't know what to say. How could she know I was here if she was not here? What do you know that I do not know?" asked Jim sincerely.

"You knew about the one person we thought might have helped her. He gave her up and took us to where she was hiding. She is reluctant to give us those who helped her. Why?" asked the sheriff of Jim, hoping it might reveal something of Jenna's past nature.

"Other than to protect those she cares about, I just don't know," said Jim.

"Does she have any history of protecting people?" asked Felicity.

Jim delving into his past said, "Jenna has been a rather shy person, not known to reveal her inner thoughts to many people. She kept everything close."

"Without telling us what secrets she may have had in the past, has she ever confided in you such fears or concerns that might alarm those of you who care for her?" asked Felicity in her quiet trusting way.

"If I think of anything, I will tell you. She was not known for sharing such things. I don't know what is in her past to make her so secretive. Do you think she was abused or hurt badly in her past?" asked Jim, with that worried look returning.

"We don't know. We are looking for answers to help her. We were hoping she might confide in you. She is now in our jail to protect her. Would you want to visit her early tomorrow morning in hopes of relaxing her enough that she might volunteer information that could help her?" asked Sheriff Hardy.

"I will try my best, in that regard, without being too obvious and give you a call after the meeting. It will be so good to see her again," said Jim with the smile returning with hope for tomorrow.

Rex and Felicity said their goodbyes and wished Jim well.

Chapter Ten

April 22nd came early as Sheriff Hardy awoke feeling still tired from the long day yesterday. Even though tired, he felt hopeful for what was to come. He decided to go to a good local breakfast place to start his day. He walked in a little sleepy eyed as he slipped into a booth and picked up a menu.

The waitress came over and asked, "What would you like to drink to start your day?"

"A hot cup of coffee will do me fine. What do you suggest for breakfast today?" he asked.

"A spinach omelet with bacon is the special today, if you like spinach," she said as she was about to go get that coffee.

"I will have the special. Before you leave, what are people coming in today talking about?"

"The same as usual. They are wondering if Jenna will be found alive. Everyone has their own theory of what happened," she replied.

"Is there any one theory repeated more than others?" asked the sheriff.

"Not really. Most don't understand why she would leave when she seemed happy here. You probably know more than most, I suspect," was her inquisitive reply.

"I would like to tell you more. When something happens, I am sure you will hear soon enough," replied the sheriff, as she left to get that order in.

While waiting he noticed his old friend, Harry Fixture, come through the door, spotting him in the booth. Harry asked, "May I join you this morning?"

"Yes. I'm having the special. Let the waitress know what you want and have a seat," replied Rex, with a welcoming smile.

Harry soon came over after telling the waitress what he wanted. "I'm surprised you have time for breakfast these days. Let me know if I can be of help. I know from past experience things come together in a hurry when you start to figure it out."

"I will keep your offer in mind. That young guy shot up the minister's house pretty good not too long ago here in High Point," responded Rex still thankful for his friend's help in the past. "How is the antique business going for you?"

"That sort of thing is pretty slow these days. The upcoming summer will probably help with tourists coming in."

The breakfast food arrived, piping hot, proving to be tasty as well. "You wouldn't think spinach in an egg omelet would go well together, but properly prepared by a good cook, it hits the spot, along with a hot cup of coffee," offered Rex, as he quickly ate in order to get over to the jail.

Harry noticing some urgency in his friend said, "I won't keep you. Good luck with your day and bring Jenna home to us."

As Rex got up to leave, he quietly said to his friend, "This may be the day we find out what is going on in this case. Wish me luck."

As Rex left, Harry said loudly enough for everyone to hear, "Have a good day."

As Sheriff Hardy drove up to the jail, he noticed Jim walking in just ahead of him. "Good timing. The chief and I will be planning our next move this morning. Knock at our door when you leave. You may be able to help us. Give her a brotherly hug when you see her."

"You know I will. I will see you later," said Jim, as he rushed to see his sister for the first time in a long while.

Sheriff Hardy just watched, thinking how nice it would be if this could work out in a way that would keep Jenna and Jim happy. As he mused, the chief saw him and said, "It's about time you got here. Stop into my office."

The first question asked of the sheriff was, "What have you worked out with Jim?"

"Last night we told him Jenna was safe and in our jail for safekeeping. We filled him in on events as best we could from yesterday. I also told him I could not figure out why Jenna did not ask about seeing her brother," summed up some thoughts he had.

"That concern entered my mind too. She had to have known he was here since her disappearance. What are we missing?" questioned the chief.

"While we are strategizing, I have asked Jim to soften up his sister to get her to confide in him and report it to us this morning to aid in our plan," announced the sheriff.

"Let's get to it before this guy from Chicago gets here. It is not that far away. We can't just arrest him without having done anything wrong yet. I am thinking we will have to release Jenna and put her in a setting where Jerry can find her," announced the chief.

"I'm of the same mindset. It involves risk, which means we will have to convince Jenna to be wired and cooperative. We will have to have law enforcement near her at all times to avoid things going badly wrong," said Sheriff Hardy.

"One of the problems is that we don't know whether he is more interested in taking her back with him forcefully or just killing her out of frustration or some other motive. Is he acting selfishly for his own gain or is he being sent here for a purpose?" replied the chief, concerned how to be prepared for both possibilities.

"A lot could go wrong no matter how good the plan. The fact it could happen as early as today makes it less likely to be a perfect plan. We have to be ready now in a way that still protects our citizens. How will we manage it?" agonized the sheriff.

"How much does Jerry Lensor know about Jenna and her whereabouts in this community? Will he have to ask strangers here to find out where she is at different times, or does he already know because he has someone here who already told him her whereabouts?" thought Chief Mathews.

"We have to be prepared for both possibilities. His not knowing much about our town and where she goes, will complicate the situation, making it hard for us to use the wire to get him to admit his intent. The chance of provocation increases as he might encounter friends of Jenna who may well challenge what he is about here," suggested Sheriff Hardy, puzzled about how to contain the situation.

"Hopefully, Jim will provide more information about Jenna's willingness to risk helping us and her. The closer to the vest her approach is, the more likely Jerry will be tipped off to our plan. Let's set up a plan that can be ready to go as early as today and hope Jenna will cooperate with our ideas," said an anxious Chief Mathews, beginning to think there was little time to work with, as law enforcement could be spotting the car coming from Chicago anytime now.

"Whether Jerry Lensor knows already where she works and lives here, we have to prepare our plan based on the fact he knows or can ask in our community and find out. If she will cooperate, we need to get her at work at the library with security around her in case Jerry walks into the library asking for her. If she agrees to be wired, we might be able to get Jerry to announce his intent. Then any action by him will give us the opportunity to act on what he does and arrest him. As it is now, we have no such authority. Do you agree?" asked Sheriff Hardy.

"I agree and think we have to have protection set up at her home as well. We need to have unmarked cars following him too. I am thinking that with the public library having so many people around her, that he will be less likely to be violent there. Hopefully, it will be verbal in asking her what he wants and what the alternative might be, hopefully, recorded. If he storms out in anger, we must be prepared for violence after that, probably at her home," explained the chief.

Just then Sheriff Hardy looked up to see Jim coming toward them and motioned Jim into the office. When Jim arrived, he said, "Have a seat with us and tell us how the visit went with your sister."

"It was a little awkward at first, but she finally hugged me and asked how I was doing. I gave her a reassuring smile and stayed quiet giving her a chance to reveal her thoughts," said Jim, as he tried to recreate the conversation, but a little unsure how to proceed.

Jim continued, "She said to me, 'I know we have not talked by phone for a while now. What brings you here?', as if nothing new had happened since our last conversation.

"I responded to her strange question under the current circumstances. 'It is unclear what you mean. Do you mean what brought me to you today or when I arrived in High Point?'

" 'Both I guess,' she said. I was a bit irritated, and asked, 'Who do you think the police called when you turned up missing many days ago?'

" 'I'm sorry you got involved. It doesn't help me in this situation,' she had said.

"I responded to her quickly with a hug saying, 'Didn't you expect your brother to care about you? Of course, I came as soon as I got the call and have been calling everyone I know to find you.' "

Jim then said to Sheriff Hardy, "I think her emotions could take no more as she cried and hugged me tightly. She then opened up and briefly told me that her stay in Chicago had been a bad decision for her, as she got to know too many men who did not share her values. She finally decided to suddenly escape and come to High Point to recover from her depressing situation. She even said she thought it had worked for years until someone she trusted sent her a note in the mail saying her life was in danger, having to do with one of her old acquaintances finding out something."

Chief Mathews asked, "What does that mean? Did she do something that threatened someone, or did she learn something about someone that was so damaging that someone wanted her dead?"

Responding to Chief Mathews, Jim, looking unhappy at this moment said, "I wish I could tell you more, but she refused to discuss it. All she did was ask me to leave and return home - that there was nothing I could do to help her. That was the end of the conversation. I left saying I would be back to see her."

There was a momentary silence, then Rex asked Jim, "Did Jenna say anything about the blood on her pillow?"

Jim replied, "Yes. I almost forgot. I did ask her. She said she dropped a glass of water on her nightstand, the glass shattering onto the bed. She picked up the pieces, but missed one. She jumped into bed, cutting her hand, and it bled all over the pillow. She was embarrassed by her clumsiness. 'Don't tell anyone,' she said."

Rex hesitated, "She seems overwhelmed by her current threat and does not want you hurt. Please go back to your room and talk with Felicity. We must make a plan after we talk to Jenna, since trouble may soon be here."

"I will do that right now. Please let me know when I can next talk with her. I realize you must protect her now. I do not want to interfere, making things worse. Do what you must," said a sad and much distracted Jim Botlin, as he silently got up from his chair and left the jail.

"Thank you for your help," was all Jim heard as he left.

After a brief conference both the sheriff and the chief got up and walked to where Jenna was sitting on her bed, red eyed and crying still. She did not look surprised to see the men.

Chief Mathews announced, "We can no longer delay asking for your cooperation in apprehending the man who is coming for you, possibly as we speak. Will you do that?"

"Yes. I will help in any way I can. Just tell me what to do," said a broken and sad Jenna.

"Sheriff Hardy said rather directly at this point, "We have a plan but could use more information to make it a safer plan. Does the person coming know where you work and live, or will he have to ask citizens to find it out?"

"I honestly don't know. I am not sure who is coming and why. I know Jerry Lensor wants me back and will do almost anything to make that happen. If I refuse to go back with him, it is hard to believe he would harm me. I thought he loved me, but he became so controlling that I was afraid to stay with him. I do fear what he might do to me and have been living with it since I left," said Jenna, as frightened now as both men in front of her believed.

The Chief now asked, "We believe you. To be fully prepared we have to be ready for others who might want to harm you. What other names come to mind who might see you as a real threat?"

"I can't think of anyone I personally know who would want to hurt me so much at any point in my life to this point. It would have to be something I heard or witnessed that did not seem threatening at the time. I have been trying to recall situations that would make it clear and have failed thus far," stated a frustrated Jenna.

"After this threat we are dealing with today, will you consider hypnosis to find that possible threat based upon what you saw or heard?" asked Sheriff Hardy, in a pleading but serious way, allowing plenty of time for Jenna to process what he meant.

"Yes. I will. Help me with Jerry Lensor if he is the major threat now. What do you want me to do?" asked a determined Jenna at this dangerous point in her life.

They spelled out the plan and made sure she knew what risks were involved to her and others. They explained about hooking her up with a wire apparatus to try to record what Jerry Lensor was saying to her, so that law enforcement would have a reason to arrest him. If he should ask her to leave with him, she should boldly announce to him she would not do it. Law enforcement would be near if he should try anything violent. If he chooses to walk away, he would be allowed to do so as he would be followed in unmarked cars. Someone would then take you from work to your home where law enforcement would be prepared if and when he should arrive there.

Sheriff Hardy then asked Jenna, "Are you willing to accept the risk being asked of you to eliminate this threat?"

"Yes," said Jenna without hesitation.

Chief Mathews said, "At this time we will leave you to have a good lunch and prepare for the day at the library and your home. Try to compose yourself enough to allow our plan to work. Some clothes from your house will be brought to you. Someone will be back for you in a short while. Are there any questions?"

"No. I will be as strong as I need to be. Thank you for helping me. Also, keep my brother safe. One tragedy is enough for our family," answered Jenna as both men left to put it all in motion.

An hour later Sheriff Hardy got the word from Madison law enforcement that Jerry Lensor's 2010 black Buick was seen on highway 151 coming toward High Point, due to arrive in about an hour.

Chief Mathews got his people together and explained each person's role. He had two of his men take Jenna to the library to her work station and placed them nearby in plain clothes armed to act at any sign of trouble. Prior to this someone at the jail helped Jenna with the wire, making sure it was placed properly to record the conversation between Jenna and Jerry Lensor. Once at the library one of the officers informed library staff to stay away from Jenna's area as something might be going on there. They were to act as normal as possible in doing their required work assignments. The chief in one vehicle and two deputies in another watched for Jerry's black Buick in order to let others know when Jerry had arrived. Satisfied that they were as ready as possible, the chief had everyone in position.

The sheriff placed himself and a deputy in the house and in position to stage what looked to be Jenna from behind, sitting in a rocking chair near a television. The deputy positioned himself to be able to see the back door while close enough to help if someone came through the front door. The sheriff planned to be near the front door to assist Jenna without being seen from outside. Sheriff Hardy knew it was more likely to be violent if it got to the house. He had arranged for a female officer not in uniform to be at the library ready to take Jenna to her house. He had also arranged to have two men near the house to cover the back and the front out of sight of the street - when Jerry drove up to carry out whatever he had on his mind. Everyone was listening for messages - alert to what could happen. The sheriff made a quick call to Felicity now, "Felicity, will you take time now for the next few hours to make sure Jim is safe and secure somewhere at your place in the unlikely event Jerry knows about Jim being in town? I don't want him forcing Jenna's hand because he was using Jim as a bargaining chip."

Felicity was prompt in replying, "As we discussed earlier, I will be armed and have Jim in a safe spot until I hear from you. Good Luck."

"Be careful. I will call when I can," responded Rex, trying to cover all the possibilities he could think of.

Chapter Eleven

This April 22nd day was lingering far too long for Chief Mathews as he kept looking for the black Buick to appear. His deputy called saying, "The car is coming not more than a block away."

The car drove past the library, slowly driving around the block, until a parking place was found on the side of the library. The male driver sat in the car for several minutes, just waiting there, sipping on what looked to be a soft drink. All of a sudden he got out of the car and felt for something under his jacket at his backside. He leisurely walked to the library front door and walked in.

Inside the library the officers made sure they were far enough away from Jenna to give the appearance that

Jenna was working by herself at the help desk, standing there looking at a computer screen.

Jerry walked around other areas of the library casing the place before going in the direction of Jenna's workstation. When he saw her, he picked up his pace, hoping he would be directly in front of Jenna before she saw him. Jenna, knowing what was happening, purposely did not look up until he was right in front of her. She quickly gasped in surprise.

Before Jenna could speak, Jerry said, "Say the wrong thing, and it will be the last thing you ever say. I have a gun in my pocket."

Jenna said, "Why are you here, and why would you need a gun?"

"Thinking of how quickly you left me in Chicago, I thought I might have to scare you first to get your undivided attention. It looks like I was right," said a proud Jerry Lensor, hopeful now that he knew what he wanted was right in front of him.

"Jerry, this is a public place. Be careful what you say or do here. Don't make a scene. Let's have a civil discussion right here before any decisions are made. Is that agreed?" said a frightened but appearingly composed Jenna, who knew the kind of person she was dealing, with.

Jerry's confidence grew, knowing that Jenna did not run from him at first sight. He was thinking he might be able to get her to walk out with him to maybe get a bite to eat and get friendly. With a less menacing face, he quietly offered, "Do you suppose we could walk outside and talk, or go to a place nearby to get a bite to eat? I'm pretty hungry."

"We could do that, but first let's talk about why you are here," asked Jenna in a welcoming quiet way, showing her charm.

"I'm here because I have missed you and want you back in my life. Is that hard to understand?" was Jerry's simple but brief statement of fact with a face that showed Jerry to be an upfront kind of guy.

"And you want me to say sure and get in the car with you, and go right back to Chicago and live happily ever after," replied Jenna, sarcastically implying that would never happen.

Jerry had seen that sarcasm before and felt only rage now as he put his hand on the back of his jacket. "You little bitch. I should have known you would be difficult. You're coming with me whether you want to or not."

"Or what? I'm happy where I am without you."

"You're coming with me whether you want to or not," said Jerry firmly with restrained emotion now as he started to raise his left hand into a fist.

With that, one of the officers approached so quickly, Jerry didn't see him grab the left wrist.

The officer, in plain clothes, now said, "I don't like what I see here. Are you threatening harm to this young lady?"

Jerry paused long enough to think about pulling that gun from his back pocket, but then thought better of it saying, "No sir. We were just having a lover's quarrel. I'm over it and will leave now."

The man still stood there waiting, so Jerry Lensor backed up and walked to the front of the library and to his car with a red face that gave away his anger.

As Jerry walked out, both deputies followed to make sure he was leaving. One of them called others to let them know Jerry had left without harm. He then returned to find Jenna crying at her work station. He then took her to a more private place so she could let go of all that emotion and fear, before he said, "You did a great job. Did you get it all on the recording?"

"I got it. I thought he might just pull a gun out of his pocket and shoot me on the spot. I'm shaking so bad. I need to go sit down for a while to gain control of myself. This was harder than I thought it would be," spoke a person in anguish with a need to let it all out. The redness and tears convinced the officer how she must feel.

He said, "You were brave today. I know it was hard, but you won't regret it. He won't hurt you again if any of us can help it. We want you to stay in our town good and safe for as long as you are here. Hang onto those words as we leave this building today when she comes shortly to take you home."

"Thanks for the reassurance. I needed to hear those words. I have lived in fear. I need to step it up a notch if I want to feel safe again," said a grateful Jenna, wiping the last tear off her cheek.

The officer then received a call. "Jerry is driving in the direction of Jenna's home. Lead her to the car outside the library where she will be driven to her home. Assure her that officers are watching her every step of the way."

Repeating that information the officer then made the arrangements to get Jenna home, if possible, before Jerry Lensor interferes. He then called officers in the library area for new directions.

Sheriff Hardy had now been informed about what happened in the library. He now arranged his deputies in such a way as to be out of sight, but readily available should things go badly. He now awaited word of where Jerry was last seen.

It took ten minutes before a deputy called saying, "Jerry has turned around heading back toward highway 151."

"Have backup ready in case he appears to be going out of town. If so, pull him over with backup. Then call me. If he stays in town, tell me where he is and what he is up to. Also, call if you see him using his phone to report to anyone," ordered Sheriff Hardy, not knowing what to make of Jerry's actions at the moment. He knew he had to stop violence, but also realized he needed to talk to Jerry to get a better understanding of the threat to Jenna.

While waiting for the return call, the sheriff called Chief Mathews, "We are not sure where Jerry is going just yet. In the meantime, can you bring Jenna to her house where I am now? Since Jerry is going in a different direction, this is a good time to get her in the house with our protection. Let's keep each other informed every time Jerry makes a move."

"Agreed. I can't tell if Jerry is acting on his own or for someone else. If he is on his own, he doesn't appear to be well planned except for knowing where she works. Do you think he knows where she lives?" asked the Chief.

"We will know soon enough. It does not appear to be a well-planned thing. Jerry has such a temper that it makes him unpredictable," shot back Sheriff Hardy.

"Would you believe Jerry just parked in front of Joe's Bar and Grill and walked inside?" announced the deputy. "Do you want me to park around the corner and go in to keep an eye on him?"

"No. Just follow him when he comes out. If he was asking directions, we can find out later. From what I have seen so far, my guess is he is ordering a hamburger and beer," suggested the sheriff.

With everyone on the job and prepared, it was a waiting game as time passed slowly for law enforcement. The sheriff looked out to see the car he was expecting, pull in the driveway, waiting for his instructions. Sheriff Hardy, making sure all were in place now, called the driver saying, "Step out of the car and go around to the passenger side and bring her to the door, shielding her from the street side. The door is unlocked. I will not show myself."

When Jenna was safely in the house, the deputy drove away. Sheriff Hardy pointed her to a place in another room. He said, "We are waiting for Jerry to decide what to do. He now is at Joe's Bar and Grill. You know him. What do you think he is doing?"

"Jerry is not a complicated guy. He is hungry and thirsty. Next to being with the opposite sex, those are his go to's. He could just as easily drive away or come and shoot me," said an angry Jenna.

The Sheriff went over the plan for Jenna if Jerry should return. Both sat down and tried to relax. An hour later the call came through. "Jerry is on the way toward you, maybe another ten minutes if he knows where he is going," announced the deputy.

The sheriff called to make sure all law enforcement was ready. Right on time Jerry drove to the curb and shut off the engine. He stepped out of the car, looked around, seeing no one, walked to the front door and rang the doorbell. No one came to the door.

Jenna looked to see that the window was open in the front living room as the sheriff had said it would be. Then she shouted loud enough for Jerry to hear, "I see you standing out there Jerry. Just go away. I never want to see you."

Jerry, expecting this behavior said, "I hear you. I've given you enough time to think. Make up your mind. Come out now or I leave and never come again."

"Fine. Goodbye and good riddance," was Jenna's angry response, as she got better cover as the sheriff had wanted from her.

It was silent outside. No words spoken. Jerry just stood there. He suddenly raced toward the car until he reached the driver's front door, got in without looking back, and drove off.

Noticing him leave, Sheriff Hardy got on the phone to his deputy, "Follow him for a couple blocks, and then put on the sirens and pull him over. Have backup there before you approach his car. Cuff him and give me a call."

Turning to Jenna, the sheriff said, "I think he thought twice about hurting you. If you want to press charges, let me know. I will have someone stay with you tonight. You might want to call your brother for company."

"Thanks. I would like his company right now, even if someone is here looking out for me from your office," said a relieved Jenna.

The deputy called back, "We have him."

"Good. I will meet you at headquarters. Keep him by himself until I get there. Make sure you have possession of his phone and a gun if he has one. Let him think about what might be coming his way. Watch and see if he shows any strong reactions to his situation," ordered the sheriff, starting to think about how he might want to approach Jerry.

The sheriff and chief then met at the sheriff's headquarters to decide how to approach Jerry, knowing he didn't break law while here, unless Jenna wanted to press charges for his threats. They both wanted to know what Jerry knew of Jenna's friends while in Chicago. There had to be more to the story than what Jenna had shared. They needed to know if there was an imminent threat. Before dealing with that subject, they both agreed that supper was a priority at the moment. Stopping at the diner, they both walked in and sat at a table, feeling like they earned a few moments to themselves to savor some good cooking. They ordered pasty with pieces of round steak, suet, onions and pieces of potato all mixed together. This is a well-known delicacy in High Point that somewhat resembled a turnover. It came served with coleslaw and a beverage. It was a hardy meal for those who had put in a long day already. Both men ordered a cherry coke for their beverage.

Julie, the young waitress, came back later with the bill saying, "That is one heavy meal late in the day. Most men eat it before the long day ahead. I take it to mean you plan on a much longer day yet."

Chief Mathews, teasing Julie as usual, said, "No one gets anything by this girl. She knows her customers. I'll bet she knows a good tip too," as he made sure she saw how much he put on the table.

"The least I can do is take your money to the cash register and return your change to you fine gentlemen," said a pleased Julie, as she went about her routine.

Both men felt like the day was long enough but knew it was going to be a lot longer, as they walked out of the diner to see what Jerry might be thinking about.

When they saw Jerry, they knew he was getting anxious and worried about things. Both men wanted him uncomfortable and upset. They both walked into the room and sat down together across the table from him. Sheriff Hardy introduced himself and Chief Mathews to Jerry and then set the recorder down and started it by saying, "At seven thirty on the evening of April 22nd, 2020, Chief Mathews and Sheriff Hardy are presently interviewing Jerry Lensor from Chicago about his day here in High Point, Wisconsin. Jerry, would you start with stating the purpose of your visit today to our fair city?"

"I think you have figured out I came to take the love of my life, Jenna Botlin, back to Chicago to live together in happiness."

"How did that work out for you today?" asked the sheriff.

"She rejected me. When I realized it wasn't going to happen, I got in my car to go back to Chicago and look for a girl more suited for me," summed up Jerry.

Chief Mathews in a friendly approach to Jerry said, "How did you ever get to know this girl?"

"She lived there a few years ago. A friend introduced me to her at a bar, and I asked her out. My admiration grew and hers did not, no matter how much I tried," said Jerry.

"Who was this friend?" asked the chief.

"Ted Donstayer. He owned a popular bar called 'Right Connections' on 77th Avenue. Important people did business transactions there. It was a little more refined in taste as was the price of the product if you know what I mean," said Jerry feeling pretty good about his connection to Ted.

"How did Jenna know Ted?" asked the sheriff.

"I don't think she did in that she just happened to be with some of the men Ted wanted to know more. She was also kind of a looker. It never hurts to know someone pretty," said Jerry.

"Who were these men? Were they important people? Did they have money?" asked Chief Mathews.

"They had money all right and dressed nicely too. Some were lawyers. Others owned businesses. One was a politician of some sort. I didn't enjoy their company much, but Ted did as he was always nearby, picking up information he could use and name drop," said Jerry.

"Could you give me some of their names so I can name drop too?" said Chief Mathews.

"Attorney David Ferind defended some rough customers for a price. Councilor George Lafferole is an up and coming politician with big ambitions, soon running for a United States Senate seat next year. Rich Knowlesko owned a trucking company. I do know some important people after all," said Jerry proudly.

"Were you and Jenna ever at any of their houses or parties while you knew Jenna in Chicago?" continued the chief.

"I wasn't the only one she dated. Some guys asked her to dress up and go with them to a couple of these men's places. She didn't like going and soon would not go anymore," reported Jerry.

"Did she ever tell you why?" asked the chief.

"Nope. She said she just felt uncomfortable around them," said Jerry.

"Why all the questions about these guys?" asked Jerry realizing he was being pumped for something.

"We just wondered why she would want to be in Chicago when she had a good life here in High Point," pointed out Sheriff Hardy.

Changing the subject, Chief Mathews asked, "Would you have really hurt Jenna today?"

"I thought about it. I get kind of angry at times. Today I got away for a while to think more about what I might have done. Then I cooled down and went back to ask her one more time. Then I knew it was time to leave before doing something I might regret," said Jerry, kind of sheepishly.

"But you have hurt someone before, haven't you?" asked Sheriff Hardy.

"Nothing I ever got arrested for. Nothing you can pin on me. I'm a good citizen," said Jerry, realizing he better stop talking anymore.

"Have you ever been paid by someone to take somebody down?" asked Chief Mathews.

"I may have been offered some big money, but I couldn't do it," said Jerry, being more careful now.

"Were you offered money to come to Wisconsin today?" asked the chief.

"I was not. Are you suggesting I came here to kill Jenna? Never. I want to be with her, not to kill her," snapped Jerry, growing angry.

"But if you could not have her, wouldn't it be better to at least go back to Chicago with a chunk of money to show off at that fancy bar?" suggested the chief.

"Who do you think I am; that is not something I could do," said Jerry, realizing now it was time to shut up.

"We believe you Jerry. What we want to know is who you know in Chicago who might pay someone to come to Wisconsin to do such a thing? Tell us that and you will soon be on your way home," said Sheriff Hardy.

"I wouldn't say if I knew. I don't want to end up dead," said a frustrated Jerry.

"Jerry, we are going to cut this interview off now. Think about those who could do this tonight. We will ask again in the morning. Have a good night. In the meantime we will ask Jenna if she wants to press charges," said Sheriff Hardy.

The night felt long to Sheriff Hardy, but he knew he needed to call Felicity before letting Jim and Jenna know more about what happened. He drove slowly to her Best Bed and Breakfast, parked, and then walked in to find Felicity. It did not take long, and he found her in the kitchen cleaning up and preparing for the next day's breakfast.

Felicity saw him approach asking, "Have you had a long enough day yet?"

"I feel as if it should end right now, but I have a few things left first. Does Jim yet know what has happened?" inquired Rex, starting to relax just being with Felicity.

"Apparently Jenna called Jim after she got home and you had left, asking if he could come and stay the night at her house, just to make her feel more safe. Of course, he did just that. I think they both need some reassurance about now. They have been living in fear."

"Do you think I should visit them yet tonight or at least give them a call?" asked Rex, tired.

"Call now and ask if you can come to see them in the morning. Ask Jenna if she wants to press charges against Jerry or let him go back to Chicago," said Felicity, since the hour was getting late.

Rex did just that and drove home to get a good night's sleep.

Chapter Twelve

April 23rd started with the sun coming up suggesting a pleasant weather day in High Point. Rex slowly crawled from bed refreshed and hungry. He quickly scrambled an egg and heated a slice of toast in the toaster before pouring himself a glass of chocolate milk. He placed a call to Chief Mathews. "Good morning to you. Does ten thirty this morning work for you to have a chat with Jerry Lensor? I am meeting with Jenna and Jim in a few minutes to see if she wants to press charges."

The Chief's response was brief. "I will see you at the station."

A short time later Sheriff Hardy found himself parking in front of Jenna's house, wondering to himself how much fear Jenna still was holding inside this morning. Would she be showing him fear or covering it up with a sense of relief, suggesting all is well?

He got out of his car surveying the neighborhood, seeing that it was draped in stillness and silence. From the reports from Officer Smith, he did know that the man across from Jenna's house seemed to know what happened in this neighborhood. He thought to himself that a day soon to come would bring on a discussion with that gentleman, as he walked to Jenna's front door and rang the bell.

"Hello sheriff," said Jim, after opening the door with a joyous greeting.

"May I come in now if Jenna is up and about?" asked the sheriff.

"She is waiting for you in the kitchen where we just finished breakfast. She probably has everything put away by now and will be ready to see you," suggested Jim, anxious to learn more.

Jenna greeted him, "It is good to see you under relaxing conditions. I feel much better today and glad it is over, so I can get back to my life."

"That is good. Let's sit down for a few minutes then," said the sheriff.

"I've thought about pressing charges against Jerry for all the grief he has caused me, but I want it to be over with forever. He is not a killer, just a sap who wants what he can't have," responded Jenna, showing the sheriff that she had carefully thought about what she wanted to share.

The Sheriff listened and thought this girl is used to living in denial. It will be a challenge to get necessary information from her to arrest the person wanting to kill her. He thought he would probe just enough to see if she might be just a little honest. "The Chief and I will meet one last time with Jerry this morning and release him. He did give us a list of people he thought you knew in Chicago. Could you make me a list of those people now, before I leave, just to see if there is any overlap?"

Jenna hesitated for too long, as far as the sheriff was concerned, before starting her list. "Ted Donstayer, Franco Darenko who visited me occasionally at 71st Street, Jack Ramset who tagged along with Franco, David Ferind, and Rich Knowlesko." She handed it over to Sheriff Hardy.

"That list is too short for five years in Chicago. There are no women on the list. What about the men you dated or socialized with? What about people you worked with at Penney's?" asked Sheriff Hardy, also noting mentally to himself that Jerry's list was rather long, but that he would also probably need to add more names before releasing him.

Jenna then started again listing names. "Sheila Harms lived across the street on West 71st Street, Cindy Mcrobe lived on South Playmore Drive near me, and Jane Chalmly worked with me at Penney's Department Store and dated guys including Fred Cummlo, Jeff Nelsum, Frank Kelzerole, and Bob Berlitze. These are more names for your list," said Jenna, now hoping the list would suit Sheriff Hardy.

"Continue making a longer list. I will get back with you after I get the names Jerry gave us that you don't have here. You realize we are not any closer to knowing who might still be coming for you," noted the sheriff, trying to bring Jenna back to reality.

"I am tired after all I have been through, Sheriff. Do you mind if we continue this conversation at a different time?" said Jenna.

"I will be going now to see Jerry. Take care of each other and spend some time talking about good memories," advised the sheriff, trying to get both of them relaxed but still focused.

The sheriff now left the house to attend his meeting with Chief Mathews. On the way he wondered if Jenna would back out of hypnosis in an attempt to find out more about the people she knew in Chicago. He wondered what it would take to get her to own up to whatever she did or knows. If she has been dealing with corrupt people, she may soon find out that such people do not forget wrongs done to them.

Chief Mathews and Sheriff Hardy met for a few minutes to decide how to approach Jerry before entering the room he waited in to see them. Neither expected to learn much more, believing Jerry Lensor to be a low level player in the crime game.

Both men walked in the room and sat next to each other, and across from Jerry, and quietly waited for Jerry to speak to better gage his temperament today. They did not have to wait long. "Why am I being held yet when I have done nothing wrong? I will be calling for a lawyer if it goes on like yesterday's session. What do you want to know so I can get out of here?" said Jerry, as sarcastic as possible.

The Chief answered, "We're happy to see you too. Now provide us with something positive so we can be rid of each other."

"That is a pretty rotten attitude for someone in law enforcement. It doesn't give citizens much confidence in the system," snapped back Jerry.

"Let's start with the additional names you were to have for us. We know of more people than you gave us yesterday. We would like to compare your added names to the list we have in front of us," said Sheriff Hardy, providing a serious tone now.

"I could not think of anyone else. Sorry," said Jerry.

"We will be back tomorrow morning," said Chief Mathews, getting up ready to leave.

"Keep your shirt on. Add these to your list: Jane Chalmly, Fred Cummlo, Jeff Nelsum, and Frank

Kelzerole," said Jerry, pleased with the way he showed these guys who he can be.

"Were the last four guys people you drank with at Right Connections?" asked the chief.

"Some of them may be, but I know them for a different reason," smiled Jerry.

"In that case they must be people Jenna dated, for you to pay attention to real men," offered Sheriff Hardy.

"That was uncalled for. Jenna dated them. I don't forget that sort of thing," noted Jerry.

"Who is the woman?" Chief Mathews asked.

"She just worked with Jenna at some department store. I think they were friends."

"She must have more than one female friend in five years," said the chief.

"She did. I don't know all her friends. At Right Connections she seemed rather friendly with Sue

Deslin, a waitress there," said Jerry, pleased that he even remembered her name.

"I don't suppose you have addresses or phone numbers for any of these people you have given us," imposed Sheriff Hardy.

"Look it up yourself. You're so smart," reflected Jerry's quite familiar attitude.

"One more thing, Jerry. Of all the names given to us, who did Jenna tend to respect or look up to, which ones?" asked the chief.

"George Lafferole being a councilman really impressed her. I think she would have gone out with him if he asked. Not many impressed Jenna. She stayed out of the limelight," said Jerry.

"Why was that? Was she hit by anyone or threatened?" asked the sheriff.

"She may have had a bruise here and there. She didn't seem all that surprised to be hit or pushed around.

She did not pick the best of people to be with sometimes," said Jerry.

"Who for example? Why was she such a poor judge of character?" asked the chief.

"She had trouble standing up for herself. She had a low impression of herself at times. Some men take advantage of such people. Ted Donstayer and David Ferind used to pick on her. Lafferole would pretend to be her hero and take her away from those guys," said Jerry.

Sheriff Hardy now stood up saying, "Jerry, It has been good knowing you. Have a good trip back to Chicago; just don't come back here. By the way, if you do hear of someone threatening to kill Jenna, call me for a reward of sorts."

"I'll think about it if I do. Good bye."

After the meeting with Jerry Lensor finished, Chief Mathews asked, 'Rex, would you like to go for lunch at the Truck Stop on highway 151 to compare notes and plan future steps?"

"That is a good idea. It is good to get back to regular eating hours again, as it has not happened much since the murder. That is something we have to work on since leads have evaporated."

As both men walked into the Truck Stop, they noticed Ed Carpenter at the counter eating alone. Rex said, "I'll get a table and order us drinks while you say hello to Ed."

"I'll do that."

Ed Carpenter noticing Chief Mathews coming his way, turned away as if he did not see him. It did not work. "How are you doing these days Ed? Do you mind if I sit down here for a couple minutes?"

"Chief Mathews, I don't mind at all. Is there anything in particular you want from me today?" inquired Ed.

"No. We just stopped in for a bite to eat when I saw you. Jenna has been taking up our time lately. Seeing you made me realize I need to follow up more on Todd Geskgell's case. Do you have any more thoughts to share with me about who might have been involved even in the slightest way?" asked the Chief, like it was a normal question asked every day as to not spook Ed.

"It is a regular topic at Joe's Bar and Grill where Todd used to go frequently. The speculation is that it must be someone we all know, but no one has a clue why anyone we know would kill anyone. If they do, they aren't saying anything," offered Ed's thoughts on the subject.

"I wonder why that is," was the brief response of the Captain.

"You wonder what?" announced Ed, puzzled.

"I mean if Todd is no one's enemy, why wouldn't his friends want to share any flaws in his character or his friends just to get at the truth?" mused the Captain, hoping Ed would consider any such possibility.

"Most people don't want to get involved in others secrets. It might come back to bite them since someone might just take offense," said Ed.

"Are we all that afraid of getting hurt ourselves when we might know something that could actually get out the truth and help someone in the process? Is the fear of the truth that much of a threat? Don't we all have to trust someone at some point when things aren't going well for us or someone we care about?" posed Chief Mathews, trying to locate some empathy in Ed, but doubtful he would see it today.

"I'm afraid I am like most of my friends in that I feel safer just letting life go on without interfering in others business. It might be lonely, but safe," offered Ed, reflecting a cautious and careful man.

"There is one problem with that Ed. One day someone will hear something you said whether you said it or not. A guilty party playing it safe himself may just want to eliminate the threat based on what he heard. Who is safe then, speaking from a law enforcement point of view of vowing to keep citizens safe?" offered one last try to get something risky out of Ed's mouth.

"Chance things happen all the time. I'll take my chances it won't happen to me. Let it be someone else," said Ed, suggesting just how much empathy he did not have.

As the chief got off the stool to go back to the table with Sheriff Hardy now, he said as he left, "Have a good day Ed. Call me if your thinking should ever change."

Arriving at the table, Rex asked, "That took a little longer than I expected. Is Ed a suspect?"

Just then the waitress came to get their order. "Hello Janice. How is your day going?" said the chief, just being friendly.

"Just fine today. What can I get for you two gentlemen?"

"I'll have the special of the day. Thank you," replied the sheriff.

"I'll take the same."

"Ed could be a suspect in that he is so quiet and protective. It makes me wonder what he has to hide. We seem to be meeting too many folks these days with that same problem. Did you notice it isn't helping them or us?" summed up how Captain Mathews felt at the moment.

"I share your sentiment lately. It makes me wonder what ever happened to good citizens. Has everyone gotten so private in their lives that they don't want to help others in trouble anymore?" asked the sheriff.

"This twenty first century technology age has left us with a lot of lonely people who don't realize a little trust can help us feel better about others and ourselves. It doesn't mean you have to trust everyone. As we grow through life, we should have discovered some people we can take a chance on to trust. If not, how would we ever get to have good friends," philosophized the chief more than usual.

"You have a good point, but the food is here. I'm starved," said Rex.

Both men relaxed now as they ate. Finished, Rex noticed that Ed had left now as others around them had too, indicating it was late in the lunch hour. Changing the subject he said, "Let's talk about what we have learned about who we need to know more about in Jenna's life. I just remembered that I have not heard from Sheriff Briggs from Chicago about the lady who worked with Jenna at Penny's store. I think her name was Jane Chalmly. I will call him today as we need to know more about Jenna's lady friends."

"We don't know much about her female friends. Maybe they will be a little more forthcoming. I was wondering about any difference in names from Jerry's list and Jenna's," said the chief.

"Bob Berlitze was on Jerry's list but not on Jenna's list. We might want to ask her about that. When we make contact with any of these people, we need to ask about what Jenna's relationship might be with any of them," stated Rex, thinking they had plenty to get them started. "I'll get started on this subject. I know you want to get back on the murder case."

Both men left to start their probably busy day in good spirits. The sheriff went back to his office to make that call to Sheriff Briggs. He left a message for Sheriff Briggs to call back when he had time. An hour later he did call back. Sheriff Hardy took the call saying, "It's good to hear from you again. Both of us have been busy."

"That we have. What happened to Jerry Lensor?" asked Sheriff Briggs.

"It appears it was more about him taking her back to Chicago whether she wanted to or not. He has a temper but doesn't seem likely to murder someone. We questioned him about Jenna, getting names of those she knew. We did the same with Jenna. I am in the process of trying to make contact with them. Can you help?" asked Rex.

"I will do what I can. Before we get to that, let me tell you about this Jane Chalmly employee at Penney's. I called her before stopping in to see her personally. She was pleasant and cooperative as far as I could tell from one visit. She felt she and Jenna were good friends who shared personal things. They went to movie theatres and shopped together occasionally," was a brief assessment of two friends by Sheriff Briggs.

"Did she offer anything about Jenna's past?" inquired Sheriff Hardy.

"She told me Jenna kept things to herself in that regard. She sensed it could not have been that good since she avoided the subject."

"In that case who did she mention knowing in Chicago?" inquired Sheriff Hardy.

"I guess this is where we start comparing names since this is where I put my emphasis also. She heard a lot about her complaints of Jerry Lensor pestering her. She mentioned her spending time at a bar called Right Connections and the owner Ted Donstayer, Councilman George Lafferole, an attorney named David Ferind and a few young men she dated, Fred Cummlo, Jeff Nelsum and Frank Kelzerole," was the long response of Sheriff Briggs, without deep comment about any of them.

"Sheriff Briggs, those are names I, too, gathered from Jerry and Jenna with little that was revealing."

"I am sure you noticed that these were males except for Jane. Wouldn't you think she would know more women?" asked Sheriff Briggs.

"My thoughts also. I came up with a waitress friend at Right Connections named Sue Deslin and a neighbor named Cindy Mcrobe who lived in her neighborhood on South Playmore Drive," noted Sheriff Hardy puzzled about why there weren't more women in Jenna's life.

"How much time do you have to find out about these individuals?" asked Sheriff Briggs.

"I have some time if you can get me started with phone numbers and addresses and any suspicious information on any of them. If it is too much to ask, I will find a way myself to get to them," stated Sheriff Hardy, in a friendly way of saying any help is appreciated.

"I will have someone in my office send it to you later today electronically."

"That will give me something to do as leads are few. If there are hints of someone else coming our way to kill Jenna, notify me. Maybe we will have better results this time. Thanks for all your help past and present," replied an appreciative Sheriff Hardy.

"In that case, that should do it until the next time one of us needs assistance," replied Sheriff Briggs as he said his good bye.

While waiting for information coming from Chicago, Sheriff Hardy made an impulsive call to Jim Botlin on his cell phone. Jim answered quickly, "Have you learned anything new?" showing that Jim was as worried as ever about his sister.

"No. I haven't. This is more of an impulsive call to you. I am still processing people she knew in Chicago. There aren't many leads in this case. With your sister keeping so much to herself and obviously reluctant to share past problems or failures, it doesn't give us much. She had agreed to hypnosis earlier. I want to hold off on that for the time being," responded the sheriff, filling in his thoughts for Jim.

"I understand. What can I do to help?"

"If your plans are to stay a few days yet, would you get her talking again about her past from long ago until present? Share successes and failures both of you have had as an encouragement to get her to trust you enough to reveal what might be bothering her. If it is so private, feel free to share with Felicity and trust her judgement to share pertinent information with me. Do you feel comfortable with this plan?" asked the sheriff.

"I will do it in as loving a way as possible without offending her. She has not shared problems in her past with me. I am concerned and uncomfortable with what I might learn. I will do it, knowing her life is at risk if I don't," agreed Jim with apprehension.

"Good luck. All of us can only do so much to help her. If she chooses not to share even with the people closest to her, her fate will be in her own hands. Remember that. You have no reason to feel guilty when you do your best to help her. We are too far into this case to have so little to go on," explained Sheriff Hardy, in an effort to put Jim at ease.

"Good bye then. I will do my best."

Still trusting his impulses, Rex gave into another one by calling someone he trusted above all others. "Felicity, I need to talk. Any chance we can meet somewhere now or later to get a bite to eat or just talk?"

"You don't beat around the bush, Mister. Are you asking me out for a date?" Felicity quizzed, taking advantage of the situation with a humorous tone.

"Now that you put it that way, I am."

"Pick me up soon, and I will tell you where we will go," quipped Felicity.

Rex did that, arriving fifteen minutes later. As he walked in the door to greet her, she reached up and gave him a peck on the cheek before saying, "Let's get a little privacy by driving to Dodgeville and eating supper at a fine restaurant there."

Pleasantly surprised, Rex nodded in agreement, taking her by the arm out to his vehicle where he opened the door for her as she stepped into the passenger side of his vehicle. Then began the short drive to Dodgeville without conversation until they reached the city limits. Then Rex spoke, "Shout the directions to me and I will follow your lead."

She did just that until they arrived, parked the vehicle, and slowly walked to the restaurant with the waitress finding them a quiet table in the back, seeming to be aware of a certain intimacy. "Here are the menus. Take your time deciding what you would like. I will be back to take your order in a short while."

Both took their time surveying the menu options with small talk in the process. With the decision made, the menu was placed on the table where the waitress would see them before she appeared again. They did not surprise each other as they each announced their order to the waitress. "Shrimp Scampi with rice and a cup of hot black tea."

The waitress smiled as she accepted the order, knowing it was special in that both ordered exactly the same thing. "A good choice" was her only comment as she left them with a pleasant smile.

Rex and Felicity relaxed with only small talk and smiles until the hot order was placed in front of them. They ate slowly in silence enjoying a treat not often had by them. They then sipped hot tea until full and ready to leave.

As Felicity was helped into the vehicle by Rex, he asked, "To my place?"

"Yes" she replied.

Both noticed the landscape was changing this late in April in southern Wisconsin as a sure sign of springtime warm coming. Arriving at Rex's home they soon found a comfortable davenport and sat next to each other where Rex now gave Felicity a peck on the cheek with a hug. She responded by saying, "Now that you are relaxed, what is it you want to talk to me about?"

"Why do you always suspect a motive when I say I want to come see you?"

"I have learned over time that when you have something on your mind, there is no use going in another direction, until we deal with what is bothering you. The rest will take care of itself. Don't you agree?" she said, matter of factly staring into his blue eyes ever so intently.

"Would you cut out acting as if you know what I am thinking," said Rex, in a teasing way.

"Maybe not what you are thinking exactly, but the fact you are thinking about something that you want me to listen to."

"Of course, right again."

"What's bothering you that you are so unsure about?" she asked seriously.

"Jenna's case is going nowhere. In my gut I feel the solving is within Jenna. I have asked Jim to get into conversations about past good and bad things in each of their lives to get her to open up in honest trust. Not having had success in the past, I have little doubt he can do it now. I need your help as you tend to be more sensitive."

"Knowing how you do things, I am guessing you asked Jim to come see me for further help." she quipped.

"Of course, I did. I need help."

"That you do. Apparently, you want to try something else before doing hypnosis. That said, it means it may be difficult but not impossible. When Jim comes to me for help, I will suggest some things to try to get at the truth without devastating the poor girl. There are no guarantees, but I will assure you I will give it my best in my own way," said Felicity, in a way Rex noticed meant that is all I am saying.

"OK. What else do you want now?"

"You know what else," she said with no expression on her face.

Rex said nothing. He got closer to her and whispered something in her ear and then kissed her gently. The discussion was over. The evening became more intimate with no need for speech.

Chapter Thirteen

April 24th arrived with Rex rejuvenated and ready to go to work. He just had to take Felicity back to the Best Bed and Breakfast first. Then he stopped at work to find Sheriff Briggs had left the information he said he would send. There were no major surprises. He knew most of these people would probably be working during the day. He also knew they had cell phones he could reach them on or leave messages. He knew who he wanted to talk to first. He dialed up the number so to speak in twentieth century dialog.

"Sue speaking" answered Sue Deslin.

"Sue, This is Sheriff Hardy in High Point, Wisconsin, calling to see if you can help one of your friends named Jenna Botlin," boldly stating his purpose in calling to get her attention.

"I wasn't aware she needed help. What is the problem?" responded Sue.

"Someone from Chicago notified her recently that someone from Chicago was coming to Wisconsin to kill her. The motive was not stated nor was the name of the notifier," said Sheriff Hardy.

"Why would I know something like that?" asked Sue, acting upset that she would be called about such a thing.

"I am not calling to give you grief. I need help anywhere I can get it. I have a list of Chicago people she knew while living there for five years. I just started with people friendly to her. She is beside herself with fear," stated the sheriff, in the most caring way possible.

There was a long pause before Sue spoke again. "I would like to help but don't know why anyone would want to hurt her in any way. Without that kind of information, how can what I know be helpful?"

"I am delighted you will at least try to steer me in a possible direction that could provide a lead. Can I ask some simple questions to just get the lay of the land where you live?" asked the sheriff.

"If someone comes into the bar, I may have to step away from the phone for a short time. Is that all right?"

"It is. I am in no hurry and my questions may seem irrelevant at times. If you are not aware of enemies, could you give me a few friends of hers?" he asked.

"She talked about a work friend named Jane Chalmers and a friend in one of her neighborhoods called Cindy Mcrobe. Sherry Halger was a social friend she confided in at times. She may have been a friend of one of her boyfriends, maybe Bob Berlitze or Jeff Nelsum, or Fred Cummlo. I am not sure which one though. Is that of any help?" asked Sue friendly.

"Thank you. I know of many of those names but not much about them. First of all, do you have a phone number or address for Sherry Halger?"

"I may have it on my phone bank. Let me hang up while I look for it, and maybe I will see other names there she may know. Give me ten minutes before calling. I will hang up now," stated Sue, as the phone went dead.

While Rex waited fifteen minutes, he thought of other questions to ask Sue. Then he called back with her answering promptly. "Hello again Sue. Did you have any luck?"

"I did. Sherry Halger's phone number is the area code you used to call me plus 800 6930. I think she works at a nightclub George Lafferole and David Ferind frequented from time to time. She knows those two men but not in a dating sense. It would be going there with a boy her age taking her."

"That is helpful. Do you know of anyone who she felt nervous or uncomfortable around or even a little afraid?" asked the sheriff.

"That is harder to answer, as it could apply to many living in Chicago, if you know what I mean. It is especially true for those running in a fast crowd looking for adventure or money. Some of Jenna's friends could be in that crowd," said Sue.

"Just take them one at a time. I will rule them out as I go," offered the sheriff, making it sound normal for us all with his tone of voice.

"In that case Lafferole, David and even the owner here, Ted Donstayer, could be in that group wheeling and dealing with a threat thrown in once in a while to close a deal they might want. I can't say that I have ever heard of them following through though. I live in a rather small circle, so I don't know anyone else in that category."

"I appreciate your help. Please call me at this number night or day if you get a hint of someone threatening Jenna even in jest. I will let you get back to work now. Thanks for your time and help for a friend. Goodbye," said Sheriff Hardy, as he hung up wanting to know more about these wheeler dealers and why they would threaten anyone. Is Jenna's problem running with a fast crowd out of her league? Did she stay near them because she was impressed by the results or afraid of what could happen because of those results?

Instead of calling others on his list, he decided to look into the three men mentioned as wheeler dealers to see who they associate with in Chicago or elsewhere. He did not want to ask another favor of Sheriff Briggs. He would find someone else qualified in more of a computer way. He thought of a private investigator who used to live in Chicago but now resided in Thraxton, Iowa. Aaron Thackerman was his name, and he knew the criminal scene in Chicago a few years ago.

He asked some people in the office if they could look up his number. They came back to him half an hour later with his phone number. Sheriff Hardy wasted no time calling him. He left a message on voicemail, "Aaron, this is Sheriff Hardy in High Point, Wisconsin, needing to talk to you about some wheeler dealers who occasionally threatened people in Chicago to get what they wanted."

While he waited, he remembered he was to call Chief Mathews today to share what they had in leads. This time the call got through to the chief.

"Hello, I was wondering if you would call. Did you come up with anything?"

"I may have more leads from talking to a girl working at a bar in Chicago where Jenna hung out with friends. A friend named Sherry Halger, who may work at a nightclub, is someone I will call soon. It appears that George Lafferole, David Ferind and Ted Donstayer frequent the place, and Jenna has been known to go there with boyfriends. These men run in fast circles and are known to threaten when needing something. I have put a call through to someone in Thraxton, Iowa, who used to work as a PI in Chicago. I am waiting to hear from him," summed up Rex.

The Chief said, "That sounds promising. I have not had much luck here. None of Jenna's friends here are talking in any way that is helpful. What is this tight connection all about? Is it protection or fear or are both the same? Are many of them tied up in things over their head, not knowing what to do but keep quiet? I can only hope we can crack one of them."

The sheriff said, "Then I will stop talking and let you crack some heads."

Not much later while Rex was thinking about how it ties together, a call came in from Aaron Thackerman, "Sheriff Hardy, It is good to hear from you since it has been a while. What can I do for you? Do you want me to see if your wife is cheating on you?"

"That might be hard to find since I am not married; however, I do have a lady I love a great deal and trust completely," said the sheriff.

"What a shame, and I thought it was a job coming my way."

"It may well be one for you. I need your knowledge and skills at the moment. I have someone in Chicago threatening to kill one of my rather beautiful young citizens," announced the sheriff, feeling comfortable with this old friend.

"I have some time. What is the story?" said Aaron Thackerman.

"There are three men in the fast track looking for success in Chicago who attend a nightclub frequently where my young lady, named Jenna Botlin, was in attendance probably with other interested young men. These men are deal making often and threatening occasionally to get their way," said Sheriff Hardy, summing up the possible plot or motive quickly.

"What are the names of these fine men?"

"Councilman George Lafferole possibly running for U.S. Senate soon, Ted Donstayer who runs a bar called Right Connections, and Attorney David Ferind," stated Sheriff Hardy.

"I know about the first two but not the last guy. Lafferole is an up and comer in the political world, and Donstayer is an opportunist who would stab his mother if he thought he could make a profit from it," stated Aaron, not mincing words about what he thought of them.

"How hard would it be to find out if these men are working together now or in the past? Has any of the people they have negotiated with been missing or left the state recently? Lastly, what possibly could my good citizen in High Point for the last few years, named Jenna Botlin, have to do with these three men that might lead to them wanting her dead? Could this be a case for you?" asked Sheriff Hardy.

"Let me do some checking with people I still know and get back with you. Then we can talk," summed up Aaron Thackerman.

"Sounds good to me. I will find out if there is any money for such a venture. Good luck. Call me soon," stated Sheriff Hardy in closing.

Sheriff Hardy felt like he was onto something now, maybe bigger than he would like. Still, he could not resist wanting to learn more, so he decided to call Sherry Halger since she probably worked nights and might be available now. He called the number given to him by Sue Deslin and waited a long time on the phone before someone answered. "Hello" The sheriff replied, "I believe you might be a friend of Jenna Botlin. She needs your help desperately now."

"I knew Jenna Botlin but have not seen her for a long time. Why would I know something about her now, and who are you?" said a curious Sherry Halger.

I am a friend and also sheriff of Iowa County in High Point, Wisconsin, where Jenna has been threatened with death. A friend from Chicago warned her but not of who this person might be. Do you have just a few minutes to answer a few questions that might lead me to others who know her?"

"No one would tell me if they were going to kill someone. I am afraid you are wasting your time talking to me," replied Sherry.

"All I want is to talk to someone who cares about Jenna. She lives in fear, and I feel like I am doing nothing to help her. If you cannot help me, that is fine. On the other hand, I can only try to learn more about her past life in Chicago if I will be able to save her," said a resigned sounding Sheriff Hardy.

"What did you say your name is?"

"Sheriff Rex Hardy is my name. I am sheriff of Iowa County in High Point, Wisconsin where she has lived for five years. My leads are going nowhere here in Wisconsin. I need to find more people who knew her over five years ago. Will you answer a few questions before I leave to go on to talk with others?"

"I am due at work in half an hour. Let's make it quick," she said.

Wasting no time now, the sheriff asked, "I know she spent time at the Right Connection and at the nightclub where you work. Can you tell me anything about anyone she knew in those places?"

"If you know that much, then you know about her boyfriends and about Ted Donstayer, George Lafferole, David Ferind, and Rich Knowlesko. Is that right?" said Sherry.

"Tell me a little about Rich Knowlesko," inquired the sheriff.

"There is not much to tell. The four men are tight and in business together. I don't know them personally and have no desire to know them," fired back Sherry.

"What kind of business are they in together?" asked the sheriff.

"I can tell you nothing up front. Nothing they would share with someone like me. I'm a nobody to them. They like to hang around people with money or the promise of money," shared Sherry.

"That tells me you don't share the same values, so what kind of business are they in?" he asked again feigning ignorance.

"It mostly involves politics, trucks, and rich people. That is all I know," said Sherry, implying that is all she wanted to say about these men.

"Switching subjects, do you know of any of Jenna's friends, or at least female friends she might confide in?" asked the sheriff.

"I have seen her talking to Sue Deslin at the Right Connections. She talked about working with Jane. I think she also had friends in her old neighborhood, maybe a Cindy. I don't think I can help you anymore," said Sherry, wanting to end this conversation.

"Thank you for your help. Please call me if you hear any hint of someone wanting to get back at someone," said Sheriff Hardy, grateful that he could get this much information from Sherry. At least it did confirm her small circle of people known. The three topics of interest for the three men gave him more specifics for Aaron Thackerman. As a last resort he thought he might contact the boy friends, but thought it risky to do so now. There were two people of interest he would like to bring up in person with Jenna.

Sheriff Hardy drove to Jenna's home and rang the doorbell. No one answered. He wondered if she had decided to go back to work at the library as he thought the job would be waiting for her. He made a call.

"This is Jim. How can I help you?" was the polite response of Jim.

"Is Jenna with you or is she at work?"

"She decided to work four hours a day to start back at the library. She will be home in half an hour. Is there anything I can help you with while you wait?" asked Jim.

"See you there in five minutes," said the sheriff.

"Fine."

The two met at about the same time as one waited for the other. They walked quietly into the house and sat at the kitchen table to talk. "Can I get you a cup of coffee while we wait?" asked Jim.

"While you are doing that, I'll ask a couple questions. For starters has Jenna mentioned knowing Sherry Halger?"

"In our sharing what has been happening in our lives, she said she knew her from a nightclub Sherry worked at. Apparently, while the men conversed somewhat privately, the two women chatted from time to time," stated Jim, as best he could remember.

"Did she say anything about what she overheard?"

"Not to me. You will have to ask her," stated Jim.

"Did she mention any other names in connection with happenings at this nightclub?"

"Only names of guys who took her there named Bob, and maybe one named Jeff. She assigned them no importance other than their paying for things. She indicated no serious boyfriends," announced Jim, matter of factly.

"Did she mention any female friends to you?"

"Sue, Cindy, and Jane were mentioned, but not with a story attached," said Jim.

"Tell me more about Cindy?" asked the sheriff.

"Cindy was a friend in the Playmore Drive neighborhood. They said hello often and sometimes had coffee together at their homes or at a coffee house nearby. She did say she felt she could trust her and left a key to her home with her in case she locked herself out," said Jim, giving the sheriff information here he would like to know about.

"Did she in any way tell you how she established that trust? What happened between them?" asked Sheriff Hardy.

"The fact that she actually showed trust in someone caught my attention, so I asked for details of what they did together or shared. She refused to continue that conversation," said Jim, suggesting he had tried to get her to open up.

Both men now sipped from their coffee cups as Jenna arrived, surprised to see them together. "What are you two up to today? Did you learn something I need to know?" asked Jenna.

Jim spoke reassuringly now to take away suspicion on Jenna's part by saying, "Sheriff Hardy just arrived looking for you. I heated him a cup of coffee. As you can see, we are just starting to drink it. Would you like a cup?"

"No thanks, Jim. Sheriff, how can I help you?"

"I have been talking with some of the people you knew in Chicago. I just want to confirm what they know and what you know regarding these few individuals," stated the sheriff calmly, as if it was of little importance.

"By now you know I don't like to share much about my relationships for fear it could come back to hurt me later. I hope it is not that important," said Jenna, showing she did not want to continue this.

"The less you share, the less likely anyone will be there to help you when you need it. Without cooperation, law enforcement does not have the time or the will to stay on a case because other important criminal activity will replace it. We are not far now from this. Do you understand why I am asking now?" said the sheriff, with that noted voice of authority.

"If it is that important, then ask."

"I have mostly been talking with people I believe to be your friends. None of them wants to hurt you. They offered information because I told them you need help since someone is coming to kill you. Keep that in mind rather than how they can hurt you," reassured the sheriff in his intent.

"Who do you want to know about?" asked Jenna.

"Name just a few people you trusted enough to confide anything personal," asked Sheriff Hardy.

"I thought you were going to be specific with who these people are."

"I could easily do that, but I want you to show me you trust me enough to share that information yourself. After you share, I will share. Does that meet with your approval?" asked the sheriff.

"If I have to, I will. Jane Chalmly is someone I worked with and felt comfortable talking with about work and things in general," shared Jenna, hoping that would be enough.

"Share a story or two of such a conversation where each of you risked something by telling me who the two of you talked about."

"At work Jane brought up how some people were difficult to work with, and I agreed sharing a story from an incident at Right Connections where Rich Knowlesko laughed at me for saying George Lafferole would make a good U.S. Senator from Illinois. I was offended and asked Rich to apologize or give me a good reason he would not be a good senator. Without a word, he just looked at George, implying there was a lot I did not know," said Jenna, showing that she did not enjoy talking about conflict.

"Did it affect future relationships with these two men?" asked the sheriff.

"No. Not really. They just continued to ignore me like most other men I knew then. I chose not to risk further conflict again," shared Jenna.

"Did you ever overhear anything about these men again?" he asked, hoping for an honest answer.

"No. I chose to stay out of their lives for my own good," said Jenna.

"Why? Were they the kind of people who could harm people?" asked the sheriff, afraid he may have overstepped.

"I can't say for sure. I just didn't want to find out."

Changing the subject now, Sheriff Hardy asked, "Let's talk about more pleasant subjects. What do you like about your friend Cindy Mcrobe?"

"She lived on Playmore Drive close to where I lived. One day my boyfriend, at the time, was drunk and started throwing me around in my home. Cindy was taking a walk by my house and heard the commotion and came running to my rescue. The two of us put up a good fight until Bob just got tired of it and left. That was the last time I went out with him. Cindy and I became friends."

"Where are some places you went together?" asked Sheriff Hardy.

"We went grocery shopping together, to movies, to the nightclub even."

"Did you ever see others you knew when visiting the nightclub or anywhere else?" he asked.

"Of course, Knowlesko, David, Donstayer, and Lafferole were seen there. Old boyfriends were seen on occasion: Berlitze, Nelsum, and Cummlo. Sherry Halger would chat with us," said Jenna, including names, now suspecting Rex already knew who these people were.

"Tell me about some of the conversations overheard on some of those occasions," asked Sheriff Hardy.

"Anything I overheard is not worth repeating. It was mostly derogatory or mean toward someone," was the short report back, leading Sheriff Hardy to wonder what stories she really did hear. Before asking more questions, he thought it might be wise to get those answers under hypnosis if he could get her to agree to it when she is ready.

"That is all for now Jenna. It confirms what I have already learned. Your sharing gives me confidence we can move in the right direction now. Believing something and proving it are two different things as all law enforcement know. We will do our best. If you have other stories to tell, share them with your brother or myself. The smallest of details can lead to an arrest," summed up Sheriff Hardy, as a way of thanking Jenna for opening up even if only in the safest way.

Relieved to have finished the conversation, Jenna asked Jim, "Would you take me out for a good dinner now? I'm starved. I will tell you how my first day back at work went."

Jim, realizing that Jenna was anxious to leave said, "Thanks for stopping in Sheriff. My sister is starving. I hope to see you soon and wish you luck on your plan."

"Thanks to both of you. Goodbye."

As Sheriff Hardy got into his vehicle, he thought it would be a good time to visit Felicity. As he pulled up to the Best Bed and Breakfast, he saw her checking her mailbox for today's delivery. "Do you have time to talk and get a bite to eat?"

"I have work to do, but I will make time for you Rex."

"Would you like for me to stop at the pizza place down the street and bring it back?" asked Rex.

"That would give me time to clean up here. Thanks."

Forty five minutes later Rex returned with a piping hot cheese and sausage pizza with extra cheese. He also had some breadsticks and a cool drink.
He walked in to see Felicity reading through her mail.

"You must be ready to eat now," he said sort of asking in a way.

"Yes, come into the dining area."

"This is nice with the table set with napkins and silverware and candles lit in a darkened room," said Rex.

"I do want you to feel at home here," answered Felicity.

In forty five minutes they had finished eating. Felicity said, "Come over to some comfortable chairs where we can talk about what you have on your mind."

"Have you had any more conversations with Jim or Jenna recently?"

"With the two of them together, there has not been a chance for serious talking. You know Jim is planning to go back to his job in a couple days as he has used up his vacation time, and whatever time his boss would allow," said Felicity.

"After Jim leaves High Point, would you approach Jenna about hypnosis. I think you can convince her if anyone can. I would like to know more about what conversations she has overheard while at that nightclub. I am convinced she is not telling us everything. Her fear may be so deep seated that hypnosis may be the way to get it out in the open. It is possible one of her female friends may have been there too and equally afraid. I would like to know if there is anything to my theory," summed up some of Rex's concerns.

"I will watch for the opportunity to present itself and let you know. It sounds as if you have an idea of who is coming our way," suggested Felicity.

"That is yet to be seen. I might be just going down another rabbit hole. I have talked with a private investigator who used to work out of Chicago to dig up information on a few men Jenna knew then. I am waiting to hear if he has had any success," said Rex.

"I have a theory if you want to hear it. The culture has changed now in the 21st Century from what we have known and trusted. Many people aren't as interested in helping others in need as much now. They fear involvement and value safety at all costs," suggested Felicity.

"Fear has not stopped people in the past from having the courage to do what is right. Why now?" said Rex.

"You sound a little old school right now. Values have changed. There are more people who lie and cheat and believe the lies. They are amoral or possibly lacking conscience. Either way there is so much of this behavior now that most people don't bother to sort out what is fact from fiction. As a result more people are getting hurt without anyone coming to help them," summed up Felicity, speaking as if it was common knowledge she was speaking of.

"I don't get it. It makes no sense to approach problems that way. If law enforcement acted that way, almost no one would feel safe. When individuals don't bother to research to find the facts or the truth as we used to know it, there is only chaos. Who wants that other than the liars and cheats who find it easier to take advantage of others without regret?" announced Rex, speaking common sense, as far as he knew it.

"I am not saying you are wrong. I'm just saying many men and women are working sixty to seventy hours a week where in the past they would have worked forty to fifty hours a week. They are just tired when they come home from a long day or night of working. They may not have the energy to deal with what they are hearing. They hope it won't affect them and are afraid if it could; it might be better to be quiet and ignore the truth or fiction of what is being said. They just want to be safe in their busy little world and let others with more time worry about what is right or fair," summed up Felicity, realizing that such a subject cannot be summed up quickly which is why so many don't want to talk or think about it.

Rex said, "I am beginning to get it as related to what is happening to Jenna. You're saying she would rather be quiet when hearing or witnessing wrong doing than risk the danger of being caught up in trouble for herself."

"That is basically what I am saying. Her world has become a very small one to live in each day. She is so deep into believing this new culture that she cannot admit wrongdoing on her part. She has rationalized her behavior as safely living when it is anything but safe. She is trapped in a fear she cannot admit.

Ironically, not acting in her own best interest may destroy her by her inaction. It is a sad state of affairs that can be helped by honestly opening up and facing the facts in her life," said Felicity, almost tired now from the weight of such knowledge.

"Now I understand the unwillingness of people to act or even discuss such ideas. Jenna must be one tired and sad person living with that kind of fear day after day just waiting for the other foot to fall," said Rex, overwhelmed himself with how prevalent this kind of thinking is now.

"One thing has not changed since the beginning of time. Not facing the truth does not make bad things go away. It only leads to chaos and destruction," said Felicity, as if everyone must know it.

Rex said, "It does not make my job easier. But understanding this kind of thinking does help me act myself to value truth wherever I find it. Right now I need facts to find that truth and save Jenna from most certain death."

"Remember Rex, we can't save the world. All we can do is act individually in such a way that does no harm but helps those in need. I might add that it is much easier said than done. Let's call it a night now. All of this makes me tired just thinking about it," said an exhausted looking Felicity after another long day.

"I am going to leave now. Get some rest. Thanks for your help. I never want to be so selfish to think you will always be here for me. Time with you is precious. You give your time in love. What could be more precious?"

Chapter Fourteen

On April 25th, Jenna woke up early, clearly thinking about how good it felt to get back to working again at the library. She felt safe at work doing something she valued in helping people without any threats from anyone. It was good to have purpose again. For such a long time she could not look behind her for fear of some kind of trouble coming. Today she planned to look only forward for the hope to come.

Her brother, Jim, had been staying with her lately. It had been a comfort to her. Last night he announced he would be leaving tomorrow to go back to work again. When she went to the kitchen for breakfast this morning, there he was dressed and ready to go with luggage packed.

"I am so glad you came to be with me during this awful time. Thank you," was how she greeted him.

"I have been torn whether to stay or leave, but know it is time to get back to keep my job, and get on with my life. All I ask is that you call and text me often to keep us close," Jim said, with a tear rolling down his cheek.

"I promise to do just what you have asked. Stop worrying about me. Have a safe trip home," said Jenna, while giving him a meaningful hug.

Jim then slowly walked out of the house and to his car and looked back one last time, hoping it would not be the last time he would see his sister. He seated himself and slowly drove off feeling sadness, yet wanting to get back to his own home and work.

Jenna, not wanting to dwell on his leaving, just started busily getting some cereal out of the cabinet and milk from the refrigerator, pouring it slowly onto the cereal in the bowl. She poured herself a glass of orange juice and sat down to eat and prepare herself for her day. Her thoughts drifted to what she should be doing again, taking a long run as in days past. She brushed off the thought, picked up her purse and left the house, making sure to lock her front door.

As she went to step into her car, she heard someone say something. "Have a good day at work Jenna. It is good to see you out and about again," spoke the voice of the man living across the street from her in a welcoming way - Joe Smith.

"Thank you for your good wishes. It feels good to be back at work again. Have a good day."

Jenna found a parking spot on the street a block from the library, noticing how quiet it was this time of the morning. She picked up her purse and stepped out of the car. She could hear footsteps coming toward her and started to look back, suddenly feeling her head slump as she fell to the sidewalk.

She opened her eyes in a fog with such pain in the back of her head that she had to close her eyes. She found only pain. "Don't move."

"What?" she found herself finally speaking.

"Please. Don't move. We are putting a stretcher under you," the same voice repeated.

"Pain."

"I know. Stay still as we put you into the ambulance," the voice calmly stated.

"Dizzy, please."

"I know the motion troubles you have. Stay still as possible until we get you in a better position," the same man.

"Try hard to stay awake," came the voice again.

Jenna awoke groggy hearing voices in the distance still in too much pain to open her eyes. She suddenly moved just a little and felt pain.

"Stay still. Don't try to get up. You probably have a concussion. Stay still. You are in the emergency room at the hospital. We are taking care of you," was the voice this time of a young female.

Jenna, heeding the warning, tried hard to not move. She waited. She tried to open her eyes just a little bit. She no longer felt in the dark. A glimmer of light appeared again in a fog of unawareness. What was going on? Then all was quiet again until noises again of people walking, chairs moving, and voices farther away like in a busy place, so far away.

Jenna awoke almost sitting now in the bed with someone touching her on the arm. "It's alright Jenna. Don't move until you feel better. Are you still dizzy and light headed?" sounded a voice she knew. It was Jim.

This time Jenna did not move her body. She just slowly tried to open her eyes to see her brother. "I can see you, sort of."

"That is a good thing. Just listen to me quietly while you are here at the hospital healing and getting scans and so forth. I will be at your side through it all," said Jim slowly and assuringly.

There was no response as Jim figured there would not be. She needed her rest. He knew his job was to stay by her and keep her calm and wait. More things had to happen to see if there was brain damage. More time was needed, more time. He knew she had not been aware of time. He could only hope that with its passage, that time would work to her benefit.

As Jim waited, he saw Chief Mathews in the hall. He took the time to go to him. "What have you learned so far about this attack on my sister? Is it the person from Chicago?"

"We are just in the beginning stages. Has she talked to you yet?"

"A word or two. In pain too much to talk. Doctors are trying to assess the amount of damage," said Jim, looking tired from the stress of trying to deal with the unknown.

"Let me know when I can talk with her. Call me if you learn more. Hang in there. Stay positive," said Chief Mathews, as he left the hospital.

Chief Mathews went to the library where he met with Officer John Smith asking, "Have you found any witnesses yet?"

"We found an old man walking his dog a block away. He did not see anyone. I have been spending my time in the library to see if someone ducked into the library and hid the weapon or her purse."

"How many people came in within fifteen minutes of the ambulance arriving on the scene?" asked the captain.

"Since it was around opening time for the library, several people were coming to work. Others were usual visitors at the library. I am trying to figure out the ones not known as well. It looks to be two or three such men. I am getting descriptions and meeting with library staff to narrow it down," said Officer Smith.

"Having interviewed many there, you should be able to get full cooperation. Let me know when you get any good descriptions."

Next Chief Mathews called on officers going door to door. Officer Jane Schindler gave him a brief report. "Two men were seen getting into their cars to go to their jobs. One woman was leaving to go shopping at the grocery store. A homeless man was seen sitting on the ground in an alley. I am trying to locate that person now."

"Let me know when you narrow it down."

With this happening in broad daylight midmorning, Chief Mathews was perplexed, since no one saw a car near the library at the time of the incident that was not already accounted for. He could not help but wonder if it was a crime of opportunity from someone living near the library. With that in mind he went back to the library to talk with Officer Smith again. Seeing him talking with a staff member, he approached John. "In your inquiries make sure to ask names of local patrons who live within three blocks of the library. No one seeing cars speeding away during that time makes me think it is someone local. I will be asking too."

Captain Mathews saw Carol Jenkins and stopped to ask, "I would like to know if you saw anyone coming into your area in the library this morning who may not be a regular."

"All of the people I saw today were regulars. No one looked different than they usually look. Even the homeless looked like usual."

"Do any of them live within three blocks of here?" asked the chief.

"Three of them do. That is one reason they are here so much. Mr. Barnes and Mrs. Harrington and a homeless guy who can be seen walking or in an alley often."

"Describe the homeless guy and tell me if he is still in the library," he said.

"He was dressed in torn jeans with a gray shirt and old tennis shoes, about six feet tall and maybe two hundred and twenty pounds. I'll go with you and look for him. He often stays for hours," she said, sounding like she was quite familiar with this individual.

The two of them walked around not finding him but also asking if others had seen him. Ben Cummlo said, "I saw him mid to late morning reading a newspaper. He must have left by now."

The Chief thanked Ben for the information and looked for Helen Hagen, Jenna's supervisor now. When he found her helping someone find a book, he asked, "I wonder if you might know more about a homeless man who was here earlier and where I might find him."

"You must be talking about Jed Nash. From your description he was here and left around one in the afternoon. He is just a lonely guy who comes here to be around people more than to use library materials.

I heard he lived in a boarded up place he made for himself behind the city garage where he keeps warm with items he found near the Salvation Army. Even they have clothing that is not quite worth some people wanting. I can't imagine him hurting anyone, although, he does have a temper."

"Thank you Helen. We will check it out anyway," said the chief, feeling good about a possible lead. He found Officer Smith, and both men left to make a surprise meeting possible behind the city garage.

When arriving near the garage, they decided to come in from opposite directions just in case Jed Nash did not want visitors. It did not take long to see the haphazardly made shelter. Officer Smith walked to the shelter first asking, "Jed Nash. Are you here?"

With no one answering, Officer Smith looked inside the shelter finding evidence of someone having slept there. He motioned for the chief to come look. Both agreed they could see someone staying there if necessary. Each of them left to knock on doors of neighbors close by to see what they could learn about Jed Nash. After the fourth house, Chief Mathews found a lady home and asked, "I am looking for a Jed Nash who sometimes stays at a makeshift shelter behind the city garage. Do you know where I could find him?"

"I'm Jessica Jones. I know of Jed. He has frequented the place for about a year now. He is quiet and tends to leave all of us alone. He gets food and some throwaway clothes at the Salvation Army. Look for him at noon each week day. Otherwise he is at the library to keep warm."

"Thank you for that information. When does he usually show up at his shelter?"

"Late in the afternoon when it starts to turn cooler. Give me your card, and I will call you when I see him," she said.

The chief did just that and went looking for Officer Smith. His information came up the same. Both men decided to leave it to patrol cars to drive by often for a couple days if necessary. This suspect as the culprit seemed a little obvious and simple, yet it appears to be a crime of opportunity, where just such a desperate man would take advantage. Chief Mathews called another of his officers to see if they had any luck searching the crime scene for a weapon thrown anywhere, or bloody clothing. Nothing was found. The chief then called Sheriff Hardy and filled him in since he knew a Chicago possibility was there too. Both men felt it would not be a long wait for Jed Nash to show up. Both decided to electronically check out this person's history before the day ended.

Chief Mathews drove back to his office to think over what the next step would be. While sitting at his desk pondering what that would be, one of his staff walked in saying, "A citizen is waiting to see you regarding the incident with Jenna Botlin."

"Send him in."

As this man walked in, the chief recognized him. "Hello Joe Riley. I hope this is good news you have for me."

Joe responded, "I can only hope it is. I did not connect it to Jenna at first. I realized later that it could be who you are looking for. I was going to work and noticed a maybe fifty year old guy running from that way in a hurry to get to his black Buick with Illinois plates. I believed it to be unusual with such a combination, so I snapped off some quick photos from my phone of him and his plate number."

"Whether it connects to Jenna or not, it is being observant of you. Would you send them to my phone, so I can get them to my people and Sheriff Hardy?"

"I just sent them. Is there anymore I can do for you?" asked Joe.

"Would you stop out front and fill out a report with more details of where you were on the street and where his car was, as well as the time?" asked the chief. "Thanks again for your help."

It wasn't long before every officer and deputy available was driving looking for this car. In the meantime computer checks were made to identify the owner of the car and to find out whether or not the car was stolen or a rental. The photos were clear enough to determine the year and make of car making it easier to do the search of records. The name of Dick Rokpen came up as the owner of the black Buick from Chicago. Chief Mathews and Sheriff Hardy met to discuss what to do next as others tried to find the car.

Chief Mathews asked, "Why would someone drive his own car to commit such a crime?"

Sheriff Hardy wondered, "Why would he not try to conceal who he was until making his getaway?"

"I know criminals don't have to be the smartest of people, but this seems too simple if Dick Rokpen is our man. Is he operating on his own and for what purpose? No one would expect to get much money in a robbery of a purse," expressed the chief.

"He has to be hired by someone else for a large sum of money or to maim the victim to stop her from speaking in regard to a Chicago problem. The payment must be in cash and the person paying unknown by the assailant," analyzed the sheriff.

"If you are right, then he may still be in High Point waiting to see if he succeeded in either killing or maiming her. If we arrest him tonight, how can we use information to trick him into thinking he has done the deed?" said the chief.

Sheriff Hardy responded, "If he is as inept as I think he is, we will probably find the weapon or purse with him. If so, we have enough to put him away for a long time."

"But we want more, don't we?" was the quick response from the chief.

"If there is a person hiring Rokpen, and that person is as smart as I think, we may get much from Rokpen and still not know who hired him."

"It's worth trying though. Time might be our enemy if we wait too long. If we catch him tonight, let's make sure we keep him isolated from others who might know what is happening with Jenna. His priority will be to know, over what might even happen to him," said the chief.

"Let's not get ahead of ourselves. Get legal where needed. Make sure we have the weapon and purse and collect his phone quickly, before he can tip off anyone," said the sheriff.

"Now we wait until the word comes of his car being spotted," smiled Chief Mathews, anxious and revived for the hunt. Now both men went their own way to look for something to eat and be ready when the action came.

One hour later Officer John Smith called saying, "I found the car parked near the Best Bed and Breakfast. He is just sitting there behind the wheel. He may even be sleeping. He is parked on the street but away from street lights. Is he just waiting to find out Jenna's condition, or is he trying to decide whether to go into the bed and breakfast for the night?"

Chief Mathews ordered, "Stay out of his view, and let us know if he moves. Backup is on the way. When we do make the arrest, make no mention of Jenna. Just cuff him and hold him in your car if I am not there. I will make sure all paperwork is there soon, so we can search his car. I will be in touch."

Chief Mathews made the call to Sheriff Hardy, "We have the location of the car with the driver probably sitting in the driver seat asleep or just waiting. The car is located on the street next to the Best Bed and Breakfast. I told Officer Smith to watch until I get there."

"I will be there myself. I have been searching databases accessible to us to learn more about Dick Rokpen. He does not have a violent history. I will fill you in after the arrest."

A short time later police and sheriff department vehicles were in position. Sheriff Hardy had made a call to Felicity to warn her to stay put and lock doors until after the arrest.

Chief Mathews pulled up behind the Buick with Officer Smith in the car with him now. He turned on the police lights to make the driver aware of his presence. Both men wore protective gear as they got out of the police car. Standing behind the car door was Chief Mathews, giving commands to the driver of the Buick. "Dick Rokpen. Would you step out of your car now with your hands raised?"

There was no immediate response. Had he awoken from sleep surprised by what was happening? The chief did not wait long before saying over the speaker. "Do not try to drive away as other support vehicles are here prepared to stop you. Please get out of the car, so we can have a conversation about why you are in High Point, Wisconsin, today."

As other vehicles approached from every direction, Dick Rokpen stepped out of his car, hands raised. Officer John Smith approached on the passenger side and Chief Mathews then stepped away from the door, gun drawn as he slowly approached the suspect. Other detectives and deputies of the sheriff's department now showed themselves without drawing weapons. They wanted to make the support obvious.

When Chief Mathews approached the man and saw no gun in view, he instructed the driver. "Keep your hands in the air until I have a chance to put them behind you and put the cuffs on until we know more about your presence here." He then secured his suspect and walked him back to the police vehicle where Officer Smith searched the suspect and took possession of his cell phone, billfold, keys and whatever else he had with him. He then helped him into the back seat before the chief drove him to the police department for questioning. Before that, all things taken from the suspect were given to another officer who would be staying with the Buick.

The man then asked one question. "Am I under arrest?"

Captain Mathews responded firmly, "That will be determined at the police station when we have a further discussion of what you have been doing in our city." There was no further discussion.

Law enforcement stayed behind to secure the Buick.

Sheriff Hardy observed all that was happening and followed the police vehicle to the police station where he walked into the station himself preparing himself for the interview to take place. All the while he continued to observe the suspect's behavior. When the suspect was secure in an interview room, Chief

Mathews and Sheriff Hardy walked in. The chief spoke first saying, "I am Chief Mathews and with me is Sheriff Hardy of Iowa County. This interview will be recorded. Is that understood?"

The suspect nodded. "I am sorry, but a nod will not do. You must speak for recording purposes," said the chief.

"Yes. I understand."

"Is your name Dick Rokpen?" repeating the address and other information found in the billfold.

"Yes. The information is accurate and up-to-date," said Dick Rokpen.

Sheriff Hardy then, in the most polite and caring way, asked, "Would you mind telling us in detail when you arrived in High Point and everything you have done since being here?"

"I came here to wait for a friend from Madison to meet me here today. His name is Chad Larken, a fellow employee of mine when I did freelance work.

When he did not arrive by noon, I called him and we agreed I would wait in my car until he arrived late in the evening," said Dick Rokpen.

"Since you had time on your hands, describe the events of your day in detail," asked the sheriff.

"I arrived around eight this morning and just drove around your fine city much of the morning admiring what a nice place this would be to live. At noon I stopped at the truck stop for lunch, and just sat listening to local gossip before going to an afternoon movie and having dinner at Joe's Bar and Grill. After that I parked where you found me and slept."

"Would the receipts for the movie or meals be in your billfold?" asked the sheriff.

"No. I just charge things on my credit card. I don't ask for receipts anymore," said a confident Dick Rokpen.

"Since we suspect you may have had other reasons for being here, then you would not mind giving us permission to look in your car, maybe just to find food wrappers or other things to confirm what you are saying?"

"I don't trust the police that much. You might just put something in my car in order to arrest me. I cannot allow that," said the suspect, now not quite as confident anymore.

"As you know we do have cameras in our community where we can track where your car has been today."

"I know," said the suspect with his head hanging down, as if knowing he had no way out now.

"Do you want to rethink that answer Dick? The next question is where were you between eight this morning and ten?" asked the sheriff.

"It sounds as if you already know, so I will not offer specifics."

"We do have probable cause to search your car based on the evidence we have. Why would you leave the small hammer and the purse in your own car? Were you that sure you could get away with killing a young girl?" asked Sheriff Hardy with contempt in his voice.

"I did not kill anyone. You must have made a mistake."

"Would you believe someone saw you and took photos, which has led to where we are now?" shared the sheriff.

"I don't believe you," one last stand for this suspect.

"I will make it easy to understand. It is never a good thing when you hit someone and then go running to your car to get away from the scene of the crime. What do you think now before we arrest you for murder?" asked Sheriff Hardy.

"I didn't mean to kill that girl. I was there to rob," said Dick Rokpen.

"It's not robbery when the girl dies from your act," explained Sheriff Hardy.

"If you have me, what do you expect me to say now?" said the suspect who just admitted to committing the crime.

"As law enforcement people in this community, we believe in justice. We want to end this as much as you must want to now. Just own up to it and be a man admitting what you did, and who hired you?" bluntly stated the sheriff, as if anyone with a conscience would do the right thing here.

"It's not that simple. I was in need of money to keep the bank from taking my house. What was I supposed to do?" said a contrite sounding perpetrator.

"It's not just about you Dick. What about the girl? Are you going to let the person who hired you dismiss you as if you are a piece of dirt? Should this person have to pay for what this person has allowed to happen in ruining her life and yours?" asked Sheriff Hardy.

"It's not that simple. I don't know who hired me."

"This is beginning to sound like a copout? You got paid something already, didn't you?" stated the sheriff in a matter of fact way.

"I got paid $5,000 upfront with another $15,000 to come when death is confirmed. I was notified with a typed note found at my door," said Dick.

"Do you have the note yet?" asked Sheriff Hardy.

"I do. There was no name, only directions."

"Where is it now?" asked the sheriff.

"I have it in my sock here."

"Would you slowly reach down and give it to me?" asked Sheriff Hardy.

The suspect did it on command, as if it was the most natural thing in the world to do, "Here."

The sheriff handed it to Chief Mathews to read aloud for the recording. "I have heard you need a large sum of money soon. I have an offer. There is a young woman who is threatening me for large sums of money. I must preserve who I am and what I have. To do that I am asking you to go to High Point, Wisconsin and kill this person in any way you choose. Just don't fail, or I will come for you. Here is $5000. If you decline, just leave the money here between your doors tonight. If you accept the money, then do the deed now, and you will find $15,000 cash here the next morning. I will call you when I know about the death of the girl."

"How many people know your cell phone number?" asked Chief Mathews, getting involved in how to solve this dilemma.

"I live alone now and don't know that many people anymore. How would this person get my phone number?" asked the now cooperating suspect.

"Let's stop a moment so that you can write down names you are sure have it," asked Chief Mathews.

In the next few minutes he wrote down fifteen names he was sure of and handed the list to Chief Mathews. With nothing forthcoming after another five minutes,

Chief Mathews asked, "Put it in categories such as business people, relatives, friends, etc."

After another few minutes he added more names and contact information. Chief Mathews then asked Dick Rokpen. "The sheriff and I would like to share our thoughts for a few moments before taking a few moments to continue. We will now turn off the recorder, ending this interview at nine p.m. central standard time." Then both men walked to another room to discuss how to proceed.

In that room Chief Mathews asked Sheriff Hardy, "How should we proceed now since he appears to be cooperating much more than either of us could have imagined?"

"I am surprised. He does not seem to be a cold blooded killer for hire in comparison to those we have dealt with before. He acts like a desperate man caught up in a situation he did not know how to handle. I suggest we hold him without making a charge since he does not know that Jenna is still alive. Let's check in on her, follow up on what we have learned and know about this man, and meet him in the morning," advised the sheriff.

"It is getting late. Let's brief him on how we are holding him and advise him not to make contact with anyone until we talk with him tomorrow. Catching who hired him may be challenging," said the chief as both men then walked back into the room where Dick was being detained.

Without turning on the recorder, Chief Mathews spoke to the suspect, "The night is long and we appreciate your cooperation in trying to resolve this problem. For that reason we are going to keep you here in a cell at the jail tonight and talk with you tomorrow. We advise that you make no contact with anyone, until we talk with you, as we are actively trying to identify and capture the person who hired you."

A tired looking Dick, who looked as if he had aged considerably just this evening, now said, "I understand the trouble I am in and regret my involvement deeply. I own up to what I have done and will help if I can. I am sorry."

Both men left now to put certain things in motion before calling it a night. Sheriff Hardy called Felicity first, "Sorry, it took so long to get back to you. The suspect is in jail now. I am going to check on Jenna now and call it a night."

Felicity responded, "Thanks for the call. Let me know about Jenna when you can. Take care."

Sheriff Hardy drove to the hospital in a nearby town where Jenna stayed now. As he searched out and found medical staff, he listened to the doctor in charge, "She is stable and in concussion mode. She is able to talk now without remembering all that happened. Tomorrow will determine the need for an MRI. Until then she is being monitored carefully. I don't think you're talking to her tonight would be productive."

"Thank you. I will check in tomorrow to learn more," was all Sheriff Hardy could think of to say before he left to go home and get a good night's sleep for what would likely be a long day coming.

Chapter Fifteen

April 26th was welcomed by Sheriff Hardy as he awoke to a sunny day, but still a jacket day in High Point. He scrambled an egg and ate his toast quickly and finished with a cup of hot tea before leaving for the office to start more investigation of his suspect. Upon arriving the first thing was to get someone in his office working on checking on all calls made or received by Dick Rokpen in the last week. He doubted the person paying for the hit would make such contact, but it was necessary to check it out. The other thing was to contact people on the list of names he gave who would have his cell number, and discreetly find out who else may have that number, without making personal visits. The person responsible found some way of getting that number and could be calling the suspect at any time to get results. In all probability that person would be using an untraceable phone to get in contact with our suspect. He first checked the cell phone to see if any messages had been left and found none.

He called Police Chief Mathews, "I think we should give our suspect his cell phone in case he gets a call.

We could have someone staying near him having him prepared with what we would like him to say in response and agree to terms given. Even if we can't trace it, we may learn if it is a male or female, and some clue of arrival of this person, or directions for us to be ready to move. What do you think?"

"Let's do it to see if anything comes of it. We need some explanation for our suspect when the person says he sees no notification of death of Jenna. Maybe we tell him our plan is to not let it out because we hope he comes to High Point. Will Dick buy that or catch on?" asked the chief.

"I am thinking we will have to have a deputy in the cell today with him to be ready to disconnect the phone if need be. Go ahead and set it up with some likely answers for the suspect to give in response to uncomfortable questions. Keep me posted," said Sheriff Hardy.

"I will do that. Later this morning I will give you a call about sitting down with the suspect again. I am trying to figure out how someone else got ahold of his cell phone, but can't find a quick way to do it without tipping off the guy we want. We may have to get some help brainstorming this one. Talk later," responded the chief, sounding rushed.

Sheriff Hardy now took the time to drive over to the hospital to find out more about Jenna. As he arrived at her room, he was greeted, "It is so good to see you here. For the first time I feel like I am aware of what is happening around me. The fog has lifted even though I feel weak."

"It is good to see you in such good spirits. Will they be doing an MRI today to see about brain bleed or any other concerns?" asked Rex.

"That will happen this morning. The results will determine how soon I can go home. I feel fortunate to be alive. Do you know who did this to me?"

"We have the man in jail where he has confessed. He reacted badly because he was in a desperate situation in his life. He is cooperating with us," announced the sheriff, reluctant to give out too much information.

"I am glad I won't have to worry about him trying again."

"Where is Jim?" asked Rex.

"He went home to shower and get some clean clothes, as he has been at my side through it all. I am lucky to have such a brother."

"I can't stay long today. Do you remember any more about the incident?" asked Sheriff Hardy, in his sheriff role now.

"I did not see him, only heard him coming from behind. I turned just enough to prevent a direct, full hit on the head."

"Do me a favor. Before leaving to go to your home, call me for assistance. I don't want any more mishaps. If possible, keep a low profile and don't talk with others now. Just rest and get better. Call Felicity and let her know if you feel well enough for company," suggested Sheriff Hardy, before leaving in order to get back to the police department and confer with the chief before meeting with Dick Rokpen again.

Chief of Police Mathews saw Sheriff Hardy walk into his station anxious to plan their next step. As both got themselves a donut and cup of coffee, they relaxed in the chief's office for a few minutes, before getting serious again. "Thank goodness for donuts and coffee to relieve some of the tension in our work. It can help us focus again," said the chief.

"I take it there have been no calls to our suspect," said the sheriff.

"You're right about that. Why no contact like our suspect said there would be?"

"I think the person laying out the money is worried the deed is not done. He probably has been following news stories before making his next step. That leaves us choices to make if we want him here," said the sheriff, unsure about how to get him here without creating panic in his town.

"I don't think we can keep it quiet much longer since Jenna is doing better than expected, unless that MRI brings up a big problem. I only want the best for her, but how can we stop someone else coming here to finish what they started?" replied the chief, rhetorically.

"I asked Jenna to call me before going home, whenever that is. We need to protect her even more now. She probably has let her guard down because she is grateful to be alive and appreciative for help given her. We will make those adjustments and try to keep her feeling that same comfort by maybe having her stay with Felicity in Jim's room. It will give Felicity a chance to keep an eye on her, but also to talk and share some of her fears from the city. Maybe we will hear who she fears the most." suggested Sheriff Hardy.

"Run that by Felicity to see if she can fine-tune it more yet. Then we will set it in motion when Jenna is ready to come home. Our job will be to have them all protected against the attacker to come. I fear he will now come to make sure it goes down the way he needs it to go. He will want it to be unforeseen by us. We need to give the impression the threat has been removed," suggested the chief in agreement.

"Let's walk in on Dick Rokpen now and prepare him to help us," announced the sheriff.

Dick had been waiting for them to come. There was a sense of relief on his face when he saw them enter. Now they went back to the same room where the interview had been recorded the night before. This time Dick stated, "Turn that recorder on. I have some questions now."

"I suspect you do; however, just remember you are no less guilty this morning than you were last night," said Sheriff Hardy, reminding him of who was in charge here.

"I want to see my lawyer right now. I'm feeling used. Why would you look out for my best interest?" said a suspect who had spent too much time worried about his fate.

"If it helps, we can charge you with first degree murder right now. Stand up and I will read you your rights, and let you sit in that cell and worry more about how badly you have been treated, after we know what an awful thing you have done," said Sheriff Hardy, implying he was no one to give orders to.

"Hold onto your britches, Sheriff. I changed my mind. I can use all the help I can get," said Dick Rokpen.

The recorder was turned on now. Chief Mathews asked, "Is there anyone out of state who would know your cell phone number?"

"No. I don't get around much anymore. Most anyone who would know it lives within fifty miles of here," he replied.

"Who might be the closest to High Point?" asked the chief.

"There is only one guy. Jake Foswits lives on Highport Avenue here in High Point. It's a rundown place, if he still lives there. We were drinking buddies years ago. Drunk, we beat some guy up and got put in jail for a short time. While locked up, we shared a lot of complaints and stories of how we took care of people who did us wrong. We both probably stretched the truth some at the time. We felt rather tight for a while and talked by phone. We agreed, if ever in trouble, we could count on each other. It was long enough ago, I don't even know if I would know his voice if I heard it," rambled on Dick, as if he was telling us about the toughest guy you would ever not want to go against.

"Have you ever had to call on him for a favor since?" asked Sheriff Hardy.

"Only once. I owed a guy a couple thousand dollars. The guy was threatening me with harm if I did not come up with the money by the end of the week. I called Jake to complain about it and vent my frustration, as I didn't have the money. He told me not to worry about it. He was pretty sure the guy wouldn't be back again and that I should just go on with my life," another story sounding like bragging.

"My guess is you never heard from the man again about the debt. Is this person still around?" asked the sheriff.

"Sure he is. Do you think my friend killed him? I saw him a year later. He had aged a lot and walked with a cane. He did not even say anything."

"What's this guy's name and where does he live?" asked the chief.

"Fred Meckershel of Rockland."

"Do you remember anything that might help us catch this guy who hired you, since you have had time to recall all that happened?" asked the sheriff.

"No. You have heard all I know. I am at your mercy."

"In that case we will end this interview. Stay put here and we will get back with you regarding charges, as we try to wrap up this case," announced Chief Mathews.

Dick was escorted back to his cell. The chief and sheriff went to another room to talk. The chief then said, "That was a waste of our time this morning."

"It may be that. However, would you look up Fred Meckershel and Jake Foswits to see if there are any arrest records we might want to know about? After that, give Fred a call to see what he knows about Dick and this story about Jake Foswits paying him a visit. If nothing else, it is due diligence on our part as sometimes the smallest information leads somewhere," suggested Sheriff Hardy.

"I want to follow up on details for keeping Jenna safe first. Then I will take some time to follow up on your suggestion," said the chief, as he got up from his chair to leave.

Before leaving Sheriff Hardy said, "I'm going to the hospital to see how that MRI came out for Jenna and have a chat with her."

With that said, both men went about their business. Sheriff Hardy arrived at Jenna's room in time to see a doctor consulting with her. Jenna saw him and motioned him to come in. Dr. Miland introduced himself and asked Jenna, "Do you have any questions about what I have said today?"

"I understand that the MRI did not show bleeding and that I can now leave the hospital to go home and rest, keeping in mind the concussion may take some time to clear up."

"Have someone with you for a few days just in case you need help. Avoid any straining. Rest and watch some television or listen to music," the doctor said before leaving.

"Jenna, that sounds like promising news compared to what might have been a real problem. I am happy for you. Anticipating something like this, I have asked Felicity to have you stay in Jim's room at the Best Bed and Breakfast for a few days. She can keep you company some of the time. I would feel better, too," said the sheriff, calmly showing concern for Jenna's health.

"It is not necessary, but I will do it if you think it is good for me."

"I do. Where is Jim?"

"He is getting lunch and calling his company about staying a little bit longer. They have been good to him. He does not want to take it for granted," said a smiling Jenna, anxious to leave the hospital.

"Would you call me shortly before being released today? I prefer to be the one who takes you to Felicity. Of course, it gives me an excuse to see her. Jim can follow behind us," said the sheriff, showing kindness.

"I will do it. Thanks."

As he was leaving the hospital, he received a call. "Sheriff, I just learned something you need to know. Would you meet me at the truck stop on your way back for lunch?"

"I will see you in half an hour."

After some delays Sheriff Hardy walked into the truck stop seeing Chief Mathews sitting at a corner table, out of the way somewhat. Walking up to him, he said, "What do you have to share? Do we have a visitor in town?"

"Maybe an unwanted one. I'll let you be the judge. I called Fred Meckershel. I could hardly get him off the phone. Just the mention of Dick Rokpen and Jake Foswits got him swearing so loudly, I could barely make out what he was saying. Apparently, what Dick told us was true. Jake broke his leg and threatened even more if Fred ever approached his friend again. That is why he walks with a cane," reported the chief.

"We have one unwelcome visitor in Dick Rokpen. I hope Jake Foswits isn't planning to get his residence here. We are busy enough," quipped the sheriff, surprised with such information.

"Sometimes the most innocent of questions can lead somewhere. Remind me to fully attend to business when I feel rushed," said the chief, with a grin on his face.

"I guess we better follow up to see if crime is a pattern for this Jake Foswits," announced the sheriff, but seriously now.

"I am ahead of you. While waiting for you for lunch, I had people getting that information. Jake has roughed up people before. Robbery is in his past too. He seems to be unemployed much of the time, as I found it difficult to find much of a work record. I'm beginning to wonder how he supports himself. He seems to have no firm residence, even in Illinois. I will check out the address here that Dick gave us."

"You have a point there. After we solve these two cases, we may want to take a closer look at his past and present activities. How long has he lived here?" asked Sheriff Hardy.

"Do you think our friend Dick is holding back something?" asked Chief Mathews.

"We are rather busy with our cases now. It might be a good idea to get a photo of this guy to our people as someone we need to be careful around. We don't want any surprises." spoke Sheriff Hardy, wondering what this guy could be up to in his town.

"I will keep looking for Jake here and let you know. Enough of that. I'm starved. Let's eat. What should we order, the special or a cheeseburger and waffle fries?" asked the chief.

"The latter should do it."

After slowing down to eat now, both men felt revived and ready to go protect their citizens. Right on cue Sheriff Hardy's phone rang. "Sheriff, this is Jenna. I will be ready to leave the hospital in half an hour if you still want to pick me up."

"That I do. See you soon."

It wasn't long before he picked up Jenna, said hello to Jim, and drove her to see Felicity. Felicity greeting all of them with a big hug said, "I could use some company right now. Welcome."

After all were settled in, the discussions began. Jim was thankful for all who were there for his sister. Felicity was grateful that the injuries were no worse. The sheriff just enjoyed listening to them without wondering about what was not said. Then he realized he wanted to ask Jenna something. "Jenna, I've had a couple of names come up in the last few days that I don't know much about. I'll mention them to see if you are acquainted with them. Fred Meckershel, Dick Rokpen, and Jake Foswits."

"They don't sound familiar to me. That last name rings a bell. It must not be too important if I can't tell you anything about him," said Jenna, a little puzzled now.

"Jenna, I know you keep things pretty close to the vest. Are you by any chance holding back on me now?" noticing the puzzled pause.

"I would not lie to you, Sheriff," said a smiling Jenna Botlin.

"You do have an excuse today. A concussion does change your reality for a while. Interviewing in concussion can be confusing," said the sheriff, with a smile.

Jim came to the sheriff's rescue now saying, "Jenna and I have a lot to be thankful for being in High Point during a time of trouble and having all this support. Living in the twenty first century, not all people feel such support from people barely known. It is more a twentieth century idea."

"Why does it have to be different just because it is a different century?" asked Felicity.

"Living in a big city like Chicago can be a different experience and for good reason. There are more people there, not all good. Some look for opportunities to take advantage of good people with kind hearts," expressed a genuine side of Jenna, speaking from experience it would seem.

"It is a different culture now with more people and technology taking precedence over conversation and warming up to people before giving a sales pitch for your product. Now it is more about rushing to make the money needed and spending more and more hours on the job. All of that can tire people from wanting to take their time in understanding what people need. Just the technology alone eats up time where conversation used to be used to gather information. Much more now is done in isolation in some cubicle or crowded room with little privacy," announced Jim, torn between being caught in both worlds.

"The challenge is there today. Technology helps us get the facts we need quickly sometimes, although we do have to fact check more, since not all sources are reliable. Of course, that was also true in past times. The challenge, it seems to me, is how to marry the technology advantages and still keep the cultural values of honesty, courtesy, following the rules, and having a peaceful conversation with different views, without arguing. A calm demeanor is still the best way to grow toward values appreciated," chipped in Rex with maybe just a little too much fervor, now realizing he just violated his peaceful, calm demeanor ideas.

Felicity came to his rescue saying, "What Rex means is that it is harder to do than to spout such beliefs. Anyone can say what they believe, but how many live what they believe. That is a lifetime challenge we all need to practice often."

"Sometimes I am so focused that I come on too strong to people. It isn't so much what I say as how I say it that gets me in trouble. I guess what I am saying is to be careful how you say what you say. It prevents a lot of problems," said Rex.

"I think you are so tired right now that you might just say the wrong thing," suggested Felicity.

"This topic is getting so heavy that Jenna's eyes went to sleep, too much weight for concussion mode. I must be going. Let her get her rest. Keep her safe. Keep that front curtain closed more. Have a good day," said the sheriff, as he left the building.

Chapter Sixteen

April 26th was getting to be a long day, as Sheriff Hardy sat at his office, thinking about what to do next. What was Dick up to? Why did he have a Buick licensed in Illinois and registered to him? What was his recent connection to Jake Foswits? Does any of it have a connection to the people Jenna knew in Chicago? Why did Jenna hesitate when asked about knowing Jake Foswits? She knows more than she is telling us. Is she a part of the problem or in fear of the problem so much that she cannot trust anyone? If Dick Rokpen is involved in other things, why would he give us the name of Jake Foswits? Even though the day was wearing old, he decided to give Sheriff Briggs a quick call. He responded quickly, "It seems like a long time since we have talked, but really not that long ago. What can I do for you?"

"I will make this quick as I know you are a busy man. We have a Dick Rokpen in our jail after he tried to rob and kill Jenna Botlin. He was driving a black Buick with Illinois plates, but only has Wisconsin people knowing his cell phone number. He gave us a name of Jake Foswits. Do either of these names mean anything to you? In my gut I feel another attack is coming on Jenna?" stated Sheriff Hardy.

"I don't know those names. I will look to see what people here may know about such people and get back to you in the near future. I'm sorry to hear this is dragging on so long for you. The longer the threat lasts, the longer it wears on law enforcement."

"Thanks. If I find a connection, I will call you," said Sheriff Hardy before ending the call.

He now decided to eat a meal fearing the night might get long. He stopped at a local deli where he could fix himself a variety of items and slowly digest that food, while thinking ahead of how to make sure no loose ends exist. After eating and watching the sky darken, he knew it was time to take his turn watching to see if events would unfold soon. He parked in an out of the way place where he could still see the Best Bed and Breakfast and the view of the window where Jenna stayed with the light on now. Others were watching Jenna's home, not knowing if the intruder knew of her whereabouts. It was quiet with little traffic in the area tonight. Wait, just wait, alert and ready. He then thought of one more precaution he could make. He called his good friend, Harry Fixture, whom he sometimes deputized in certain situations. "Harry, I have a special assignment for you tonight, if you are up for it."

Harry said, "It must be right now if that is your first thing you say to me. What is it?"

"Bring your gun and consider yourself deputized. I want you to go to Felicity's Best Bed and Breakfast now to stay with her, Jenna and her brother out of the way of the windows. There could be some shooting. I will be a short distance away in my car, waiting for the attempt on Jenna's life. Keep them calm. Felicity knows about other plans made there."

"I will be right there. Stay safe," said Harry to his best friend now.

Half an hour later Rex watched as Harry drove up and parked his car in front of the Best Bed and Breakfast. He casually got out and walked in the front door to see Felicity staring at him from around a corner with a gun in her hand.

"I am here in peace," said Harry, with his usual humor. "Don't shoot."

"Come in and help protect us then, if you must. We are being cautious not knowing if anything will happen tonight," stated Felicity, in her serious tone.

Outside Sheriff Hardy and other law enforcement continued to watch and wait. At midnight reports started coming in of seeing a black Ford Edge circling Jenna's home, then proceeding toward the bed and breakfast, where the driver parked a couple blocks away, and just sat there.

Vehicles now drove to position themselves for quick movement in that area. All patiently waited to see what might be coming next. Ten minutes later a man was walking toward the bed and breakfast casually, noticing no one in the area outside of their homes and few lights on in houses. From a side street he finally approached the room Jim had been staying in, walking to the window with shades partially closed. To someone going by in a car, he would have appeared to be a peeping tom. It was evident he was not, as he pulled a Glock from inside his jacket, rapidly firing half a dozen shots through the window. He just as quickly turned and ran down a side street.

Sheriff Hardy waited until the shooter got to the street where the Ford Edge was parked. He gave the order, "Converge on the vehicle with lights flashing and guns drawn."

Chief Mathews was first to arrive and act, opening his door, using a bull horn, and saying, "Get out of your car now, drop your gun slowly, and raise your hands above your head."

Nothing happened. Just when Chief Mathews was about to make the announcement again, the suspect opened the door, dove out onto the ground onto his belly, with Glocks in both hands, firing rapidly.

While the chief got back into his vehicle to avoid the bullets, others returned fire, until movement stopped. The intruder lay on his belly now, quietly, as police and sheriff deputies approached, with guns still drawn. Noticing the two Glocks on the ground, both were picked up and bagged carefully. Officer John Smith now felt for a pulse. He announced, "He is still alive." Then he carefully searched the man lying on the ground, putting all loose items into baggies. Sheriff Hardy now approached. He proceeded by making a call. "Send an ambulance to 210 West Bradley Street for a man shot in lower extremities."

The sheriff asked, "Has anyone other than the suspect been shot in the exchange of gunfire?"

"One of the officer's said, "I was hit in the crossfire in my left upper arm."

Sheriff Hardy said, "Have one of our personnel help you until the ambulance gets here. The rest of you wait until the ambulance is gone before examining the Ford Edge. Chief Mathews, will you take over here as I go back to the bed and breakfast? I want the suspect guarded until we have a chance to talk to him."

Chief Mathews responded, "Don't worry about anything here. I've got it. I will photograph the scene and take care of necessary details."

The sheriff made one more call before leaving. "Harry, is anyone injured?"

"No. We hid as you instructed us."

"I am on my way over to you now. The intruder has been shot and is being taken to the nearest hospital," explained the sheriff.

The sheriff drove back to check out the scene of the shooting next. He took necessary personnel with him to photograph, as soon as he had a chance to briefly look for himself. Arriving, he met Harry Fixture at the door, asking, "How is Jenna handling all of this?"

"With the preparation taken, she is not as shaken as you would expect. She is still feeling the effects of the concussion. Jim and Felicity have been a calming influence."

Before talking to anyone else, the sheriff looked briefly outside the window, where the suspect shot from, to see if anything may have been dropped, looking for shell casings and direction of shots fired. He then went into the room just enough to see the amount of damage done and to gage the proficiency of the shooter. He appeared to be an expert shot showing experience. Now he went to talk to the people nearest to the shooting.

Hugging Felicity, he looked her in the eyes, seeing some tears, and said, "Are you handling all of this? It is a lot to ask of you and Harry and Jim and Jenna."

Being quiet for Felicity, she only said, "We all did what we were instructed to do, knowing you were protecting us. No one likes facing danger and our mortality. I hope none of us has to ever do it again."

Walking over and hugging Jenna and Jim, Rex calmly said, "I hope this is the end of it. We hope to find out a lot more in our interrogation. We will take your statements soon. For now sit and talk among yourselves, and try to get some sleep. Harry and Felicity will look after you. Thanks for your cooperation."

The rest of the early morning hours were spent following proper protocol and making sure safety was assured. The media and newspaper people were asking for explanations and interviews. He and the chief would be busy before getting a chance to sleep. He called the chief now. "Is it alright with you if we meet with the media at the police station shortly, and agree about how much we want to give them yet this morning?"

"Your people and mine are doing their jobs protecting the scene. The injured are being cared for, and the attacker is in the hospital with guards with him until we get to talk to him. Even awake, he is saying nothing," said the chief.

"That does not surprise me. Will he make it through surgery?" asked Sheriff Hardy.

"He will. He took some shots in the legs and butt. He will be hurting but will recover. The medical staff will call us when they think he can answer questions," announced Chief Mathews.

"Let the media know where to meet. I think we know what we need to say. I will see you in a few minutes."

Before beginning the press conference, both men agreed not to give out the shooter's name. The press conference began with a local news reporter asking, "Was anyone killed tonight in High Point?"

Chief Mathews took the question. "A local man appears to have attempted to kill someone, but did not succeed. He was shot several times and a local police officer was shot in the arm. They will survive."

"Who was the intended target?"

"It was someone recently staying at the Best Bed and Breakfast. We will provide more details later," said Chief Mathews.

"How safe is the public?"

"We do not know of other threats at this time. It appears to be the actions of one man who we have in custody. Further interrogation may give us more information in that regard," said Sheriff Hardy, calmly.

"If anyone has information that might in anyway explain what happened here, please contact the sheriff's department of Iowa County or the High Point Police Department," said Chief Mathews, ending the interview process for the time being.

After completing other necessary items in preparation for calls later in the morning, both men finally drove home to the comfort of their own beds, before awaking to greet another day.

Chapter Seventeen

The 27th of April 2020 began late for Sheriff Hardy, as he arrived at his office at 9:00 a.m. with reporters waiting. He met them saying, "I am going to ask you to wait until noon before asking questions, as I need the time to follow up on happenings earlier this morning. That way I may have more to give you. Thank you for your patience. Chief Mathews and I are doing our best to bring all the facts together."

Sheriff Hardy then called Chief Mathews, "Good morning, Chief. What time did you get here this morning?"

"9:00 a.m. started my day. How should we proceed?"

"Let's meet with our people to get updated. Then the two of us should compare notes and prepare to meet the press at the sheriff's office, if that meets with your approval," said Rex.

"Sounds good to me. See you in an hour."

When they met, they pooled their information and did a dry run prior to the press conference. "The perpetrator was the man we have come to know now in our community to be Jake Foswits, who has lived here for a short time. Since his surgery this morning, he is resting in recovery at the local hospital with police supervision. We will have to wait for some recovery to tie him to Dick Rokpen. As you probably know by now, with all the excitement in High Point, even Dick Rokpen knows that Jenna is alive and well. His resentment is noted. My officer was treated at the hospital and sent home," reported the chief.

"Evidence has been collected and properly recorded. The scenes at the shooting sites have been photographed and documented. People at both sites are being interviewed for their statements. When things slow down, I want to talk with Jenna again to see how these two men may be connected to her. We need to gather more information on the whereabouts of Jake Foswits here, also for his past places of residence, employment, possible crimes, criminal connections of any sort, and possible connections to Chicago," announced Sheriff Hardy.

"How much can we share with the press in the next few minutes? asked Chief Mathews.

"We have to share the shooter's name, residence here, and facts of his surgery and recovery time before we can talk to him. We can ask citizens to share any knowledge of his acquaintances or conversations with local people. We have no motive as yet confirmed," said the sheriff.

"We have the person who attacked Jenna on the sidewalk recently, in jail, awaiting charges. His name is Dick Rokpen. If anyone can help us make a connection between Dick Rokpen and Jake Foswits, please call us to see if there is a common motive," said Chief Mathews.

"Let's go meet the press and each of us share what we just agreed to," said Rex.

At noon the announcement was made to the satisfaction of reporters who had been patiently waiting for news to report to worried and interested citizens. Obvious questions were asked by reporters afterward. Is Jenna in further danger? Could more men be coming to High Point to do harm? What has she done to cause payback? What can the public do to help find out more about Jake Foswits?

"Law enforcement has no answers to such questions. We are looking into anything and everything that will give us leads to solve these events. The public's help is needed. The narrative will become clear over time. It is early stages," explained the sheriff.

After lunch Rex decided to stop and visit with Jenna, if she was up to it, while he waited to hear from the hospital as to Jake's waking up for some brief questions. He now walked into the new room Jim and Jenna were occupying, after a brief knock on the door. "How are you both doing today? Have you finished your statements?"

"We have. We both want to thank you again," announced Jenna.

"It looks like I am having a difficult time leaving Jenna. Maybe I should just move here," said Jim.

"Have you two had any time to share incidents in your lives?" asked Rex, just being friendly.

"I have asked Jenna what contact she has had with either or both men trying to kill her," said Jim.

Jenna said, "I am recovering from the concussion and still find little I can recall about either of them."

"I am glad you said little, because that little bit is more than we know now. Fill me in on the little things please," said Sheriff Hardy, anxious to hear more.

"I don't know anything about Dick Rokpen. Jake Foswits is familiar to me in some way. I think he was at the nightclub in Chicago one time when I was there with a boyfriend, Jeff Nelsum. I only went out with Jeff once," said Jenna, trying to recall.

"I hate it when someone stops in the middle of a story," mused Rex.

"I guess I am not a good story teller. I met Jeff at 'Right Connections'. He worked once in a while for Ted Donstayer doing odd jobs, as he put it to me.

One day, I was sitting at a table talking to Sue, who worked there, as you know. We were just chatting and laughing when Jeff walked up and started sharing his life with me. That is when I learned about what he did for Ted. He said it helped pay his bills, but wasn't always ethical. He always reminded me that life wasn't fair. I didn't want to know any more, so I just talked to him about day to day things. Jeff was rather simple but nice at times. One day he asked me to go to the nightclub with him. In a weak moment, I said yes," said Jenna. "This is kind of boring, isn't it?"

"Not at all. You got my interest. Let's hear the rest of it."

"There isn't much left. He picked me up at Right Connections the next night, all dressed up, trying to impress me. When we arrived, he started treating me to expensive drinks and food. I asked him how he could afford such a place. He just said it was part of doing business with Ted. I cut him off, since I didn't want to know more about Ted. Ted was known for cutting corners in his life. I didn't feel comfortable around his friends. Anyway, later in the night, while

Jeff was talking with another young lady, I just walked around observing others and listening to conversations to see what others were like who came. I heard a woman mention Ted's name and decided to listen for a couple minutes. They implied he made money by moving young girls. That's when Jeff came up behind me and tickled me, asking me what I was up to. I just said I was bored and started walking around. He didn't like that much and asked if I knew the people who were talking when he came up and tickled me. I suggested there was no reason for me to know them and asked if he could take me home. He said no more and took me home. End of story," said Jenna.

"I don't get it. What does it have to do with Jake Foswits?"

"Oh. I guess I forgot that part. Jake was one of the guys in the group I overheard talking," said Jenna, as if it was the most unimportant detail in her life. She looked at Rex, with that puzzled look on her face again, as if she wanted to ask Rex a question.

"Did you want to ask me something?" asked Rex.

"No. Why?" said Jenna.

"I got the impression you overheard a conversation you were not meant to hear. It might be important, and it might not. What do you think?" asked Rex, wondering to himself if something was starting to click in that mind of hers, or if it was just one more thing to suppress, as if it never happened. Jenna might not know what to do with this information, but Sheriff Hardy knew.

"I'm tiring you out Jenna. I am going to get back to work so you can get some rest," said Rex, as if it was just another pleasant conversation.

As Rex left, he knew what was coming next for him. In his car he called Chief Mathews. "Chief, I think I just learned a small piece of information that might just give us some direction."

"What might that be?"

"I'm coming to share what I just learned. Before I get there, would you look up the name of Jeff Nelsum, an acquaintance of Jenna's in Chicago? I suspect he has a checkered past. It is probably a connection to why people from Chicago are out to kill her," said Sheriff Hardy.

A few minutes later, the two men met at the police station where Rex told the chief the story told by Jenna. The chief listened to it carefully taking in what had just transpired. "You're saying she did not see the connection, as an important possible connection, to someone trying to kill her twice in the last few days? I don't believe it."

"Believe it or not, Jenna has an amazing ability to run from problems. She still hasn't understood that it is probably killing her. I hate to say it, but I suspect that many people in our society live that way every day, just like she does, but without such drama. Someone needs to have a conversation with that girl even though it might not even register. Someday she will learn it's no way to live life. Ignoring facts can only lead to chaos," replied the sheriff.

"I did learn something about Jeff Nelsum. In his young life he has been involved with undesirable people in working for them, whatever the price. He has a habit of making wrong choices over and over again. He has been bailed out of jail more than anyone I know. Someone knows how to use him for their own welfare," said Chief Mathews, with a growing awareness of what is happening in High Point.

"He and Jake Foswits need to be looked at in great depth, probably for a long time. I think I see their future in prison. Could I be wrong?" mused Sheriff Hardy, projecting the use of days to come.

"Let's get as much information on them as we can before that serious conversation with Jake," suggested the chief.

The phone ringing for Sheriff Hardy soon was to notify both men where they were going next. Half an hour later, they were walking into Jake Foswits room at the hospital to the sight of a most uncomfortable looking person, lying on his stomach due to the surgery on his butt, with legs twisted in an uncomfortable position after surgery.

Sheriff Hardy couldn't resist saying, "Jake, you don't look that good."

Jake looked toward the door seeing the men. "Thanks to you."

"You made a bad choice trying to shoot it out with so many of us. You clearly were outgunned," said Chief Mathews, now catching on to Rex's humorous trait.

"It's not funny, and I have nothing to say. I'm in too much pain."

"That is the truth. Murdering people brings much more pain," said Sheriff Hardy, almost smiling.

"I didn't murder anyone. I just felt like having fun with my new gun; expensive play," said Jake.

"You have a pretty good sense of humor for someone in so much trouble," announced Chief Mathews.

"I'm suddenly tired. Come back another time," announced a weary Jake.

"We will be back to finish what you started later," said Sheriff Hardy as both men walked out the door. Outside, before talking to the doctor, they wondered if they might have been too hard on him. Then they both thought better of that as they walked up to the doctor.

"I'm Sheriff Hardy and this is Chief Mathews. How soon will it be before we get a chance to interrogate this criminal named Jake?"

"He's a tough guy and pretty cranky. If you can do it here, tomorrow might be more productive as the drugs are making him drift more today," suggested the doctor.

"We will call before coming tomorrow. Thanks."

Outside of the hospital Chief Mathews asked, "What do you make of this Jake? Does he really think he is going to get out of this crime?"

"I'm not sure. He seems like a tough guy whose life has caught up with him. He probably is just looking at the end of life as he knows it. If so, it might help us get to him to maybe rectify some wrongs. I think he responds to humor. Let's use it tomorrow to appeal to his good side, if he has one. Good cop, bad cop, may work here," said Sheriff Hardy.

"Before tomorrow, I want to contact Sheriff Briggs again, with our news of the arrest of two people who have tried to kill Jenna, but more urgent right now, is to find out about trafficking young girls in Chicago, or here, as overheard by Jenna listening to Jake. I'll fill you in later," said the sheriff.

"I'll catch you later then. Good luck."

Back at his office Sheriff Hardy made the call. Once again he had luck getting hold of him. "Sheriff Hardy. It seems like we speak often these days. I'm guessing you have messages for me this time. Am I right?"

"Yes I do and also questions for you regarding information I have just learned about your area in terms of trafficking young girls. I'll start with two attempts on Jenna's life here. The first was an attack on the street by a Dick Rokpen who was caught and is spending time in our jail. The second was early this morning by Jake Foswits shooting several rounds in an attempt to kill Jenna. We shot him, leaving him in the hospital here, where we will interrogate him tomorrow. Again, do those names mean anything to you?"

"It sounds as if they should. Maybe I just didn't dig far enough when you asked me earlier. How did you hear about Jake?" asked Sheriff Briggs.

"First of all, in interrogating Dick, he mentioned knowing this guy and asked for his help when another man threatened him over money owed. Jake told him not to worry about it and that he would deal with it. Dick never heard more from the man threatening him. Then later Jake notified him about returning the favor after hearing that Dick was about to lose his house, due to lack of money. He apparently gave him cash to kill Jenna and promised a large amount when the deed was done," said Sheriff Hardy.

"I will try to work with that extra information to learn more. How did you learn about child trafficking?"

"Today I visited Jenna, to ask more about Jake, and I asked her to remember even the smallest incident with him. She told this long drawn out story of a Jeff Nelsum, who dated her and took her to this Chicago nightclub, and left her to talk with another young girl. She then just wandered around until she heard Ted Donstayer's name mentioned in group conversation. Interested, she listened in to talk of trafficking of young women. Absentmindedly, she admitted Jake was in the group she listened to," as Rex summed up the rest of Jenna's story.

"I have contacts at that nightclub. I think I can work with that to flesh this out enough to get a lead if this is happening here, or in your neighborhood. I will do what I can. Thanks for calling," said Sheriff Briggs, before he ended the call.

With so little sleep last night, Rex was feeling weary and knew his productivity was about to lessen. Too early to sleep, he called Felicity. "Do you by any chance feel like going out for supper with me now? I am feeling rather tired from the long night."

"Yes. Of course I will eat with you and even put you to bed afterwards if you like. Stop by and pick me up and surprise me," Felicity said and cut the call short.

Rex was too tired for a speedy comeback. He arrived soon after the call to find her waiting for him. "That was quick. Which part of my statements created such a speedy response?" said Felicity.

Rex only responded by helping her into the vehicle. They ended up at the local truck stop because it would be quick. They both ordered the special of the day, in silence, before engaging in conversation on the way back to the Best Bed and Breakfast.

"You are really tired Rex. Maybe you should just drop me off and go home to get some sleep," she said.

"I wanted to talk with you about something first." He then told her Jenna's story this afternoon.

"That is interesting. I see where it may help you crack this case eventually. I hope it also gets the people trafficking children," she said.

"That's not the part I wanted to talk about."

"Be more clear. What am I missing?" she said.

"Jenna's approach to living her life with her head in the sand," Rex responded.

"A large part of our population does that Rex. Are you looking for a way to help her or the many who have the same problem and don't know it?" she stated, rather succinctly this time.

"Yes. It is so sad. It trivializes her life. She may live and die never knowing the richness of life. Her approach leaves no room for growing as an individual to know what is worth doing that makes a difference to her and others."

"That is correct but not necessarily right, is it?" she said.

"Forget about everybody. How can we help one somebody named Jenna?"

"One person we can help if she wants the help. We may have to point out the instances where she ignores the facts, and simply ask her if that is all she wants of life. When she asks what we mean, we may have to tell her about the richness of our lives and explain the effort it takes to get that richness, where people become so important to us, and how it makes all the difference in the world. If that does not register with her, we may have to use her own approaches, to point out how ignoring the facts of life does nothing to enrich life," said Felicity.

"I'm glad we had this talk. I am too tired to get any more out of this conversation. I must say good night now, to prepare for tomorrow's interrogation of Jake. Good night."

He walked her to her door, walked back to the vehicle, drove home and moments later was sound asleep on his davenport.

Chapter Eighteen

April 28th was a bright and sunny day, signaling spring and warm weather again. Rex awoke, rested ready to tackle his day. He started it with his usual scrambled eggs, toast and a cup of coffee. As he drove to the hospital, his thoughts turned to Jake Foswits and his association with Dick Rokpen, wondering how many other people they knew both in Chicago and in High Point. He hoped to soon find out as he walked in to greet Chief Mathews. "Hello chief, are you ready to see what we can get out of Jake now?"

"Let's start with a soft approach to try to gain some rapport to see if there is a soft side to this criminal. Most of us have someone in our lives who saw the good in us. Who might that be for Jake?" said Rex, as he now entered the hospital room where Jake now resided uncomfortably.

"How are you this morning Jake?"

Jake's face showed a reluctance to say anything, then he thought better of it, saying, "For the circumstances

I am in, I could be worse off. I have pain and feel groggy from the drugs."

"From our point of view neither of us wanted you dead. It is not something we would want to be responsible for. Unfortunately, you gave us little chance to avoid what happened. We just want our community to return to its peaceful state again. We hope you will help us accomplish that," said Rex.

"I'm not sure I am able to help you there. I am not a big player in anything here," assured the criminal, looking for any possible way out of his situation.

Chief Mathews now entered into the conversation. "We don't know much about you personally since you have only lived here a short time. Did you grow up in Wisconsin? Tell us about some of the good things you remember growing up."

"I grew up not far from here some twenty five miles south in Thraxton, Iowa."

"Just to get to know you better, start with where you were born and some of the good experiences in your life. We want to get to know that part of you," suggested the chief.

Jake hesitated unsure just how much he wanted to reveal. He then started to think more about his situation and determined what he could lose. He needed help from these men now. "I was born there and stayed for the first twenty years of my life. My father was an alcoholic, and my mother left him when I was fourteen. Life got rough then, but I still had friends in high school that got me through, until I could leave home and take care of myself."

The chief followed up with, "You had a tough childhood. Who were the people in Thraxton that were there for you?"

"I made some poor choices too in school, meeting people not good for me, leading to small crimes. I don't see them anymore. A couple friends from school befriended me and took me to movies with them. I had some double dates then and met a couple nice girls. Trish Collins, a local Thraxton girl, was kind to me and helped me realize such people do exist. Then she went off to college. That's it for upbringing," said Jake, recalling some pleasant times in his youth.

"Can you share any times in your life where that kindness Trish showed you carried over to help someone?"

"Later when I moved to Chicago, I saw an old guy just walking down the street get attacked by some young teens. He couldn't defend himself, so I punched a few of them enough so that they ran away. The old guy thanked me and offered me a twenty. I told him to forget it. I didn't like people taking advantage of someone unable to defend themselves," stated Jake, with a small tear in his left eye.

"Have you ever regretted helping that old man?"

"Nope"

"Jake. That's the kind of thing that shows who you really are. Is that why you helped Dick with his troubles?" asked Sheriff Hardy.

"I suppose so."

"Now I know why I saw something I liked in you at the hospital. You've got spunk Jake. You would help someone in need even when getting you in trouble. You have character when you are being yourself," said the sheriff, with some sincerity and a belief that most people have some good in them.

"I see some truth in what you are saying, but what I have to do to survive can rub away that side of me in a hurry," said Jake.

"We want to give you a chance to rub aside that part of you that's hard for you to live with. If you come clean with us, we can help you with the charge against you in High Point," said Sheriff Hardy in the most serious of soft tones.

"You caught me in the act. I am not going to walk away."

"You will do some time for this, but how much is up to you. Your good side can help salvage your life and make that young girl who was kind to you proud of you. Just be honest with us today," said Chief Mathews.

"You could also be setting me up to spend the rest of my life in prison. Maybe this is the time where I want to see an attorney."

"You could be right. Then we would ask for the maximum sentence, but that is not our way in Wisconsin. We believe in second chances when the situation warrants it. Make your choice based on the best part of yourself. You have seen where the bad side has led you. Decide now what you really want. Will the people with the money be there for you, or will they cut connections or take their revenge on your failure?" said Sheriff Hardy.

"What are you wanting if it is not just this case?"

"I think you know. It is about Chicago and taking those people out of society, so others can live good lives," said Chief Mathews.

"I want to be honest with you, but first show me the crime," said Jake, testing now to see if the Chief was telling the truth or just guessing.

"Trafficking young girls."

Jake now stopped to think. "You appear to know more than I thought was possible. You're willing to help me if I give them to you."

"That's what we're saying Jake. It's the point where you turn that life around to something you can be proud of. It's in your hands now," said Chief Mathews, hoping against hope that it might happen, that this man was not as evil as previously thought.

"I do want to salvage something of my life. It's not well lived yet. I will tell you what I know and hope it is enough."

"Start from the beginning by putting it in words on this tablet I am now giving you. Take your time while the two of us step out to let you think clearly and completely. Both of us can see you are tiring and need to rest. Sleep if you have to now. When you wake up, write down everything. Just finish it as best you can. Then call for the nurse. She will get in touch with us. Give us what you know about the trafficking operation. We will deal with your High Point involvement later when we have a better idea how to help you," announced Sheriff Hardy as both men now walked out leaving Jake.

The two men found a room to sit and talk wondering if this was a vain effort. They could only hope it was not. Stranger things have happened. The Chief said, "You noticed he was free to talk about personal things even though he knew we had the recorder going."

"I think we were able to see some of that helping character in him. He now saw himself in a situation only bad. That left him needing hope more so than ever before. Loss of hope was well known; he needed no more of that. He understood what we were talking about in terms of kindness. He had a choice. Now we see if he has the courage to act on it," said Sheriff Hardy.

The chief now left to get back to the police station. Sheriff Hardy wanted to know if someone else knew some of what Jake was talking to them about. He drove off to find out.

After stopping at home to fix himself a sandwich, have some fruit, and something to drink, he silently thought more about how quickly things could happen. With that in mind he drove to the Best Bed and Breakfast and knocked on Jenna's door.

Recognizing the voice Jenna said, "Come in,"

After some small chit chat, he just came out with it. "Jenna, what do you know about Jake's childhood?"

"I don't know much as I don't know Jake well. All I know is what I heard from Jeff Nelsum and others who came to Right Connections to drink their problems away. He grew up in Iowa and came to Chicago shortly after high school to find work. Not having much luck, the people who frequented Right Connections soon gave him the wrong connections until he was at their mercy, because he needed the money."

"Did he or someone else ever tell you about any important people in his life?" asked Rex.

"Trish Collins from Iowa is the only one I ever heard about. She was the angel in his life back in Iowa. No one knows much more. I think he wanted to protect his memory of her, a symbol of some kind," said Jenna, with a smile on her face possibly reflecting on some past memory of her own.

"I have one last question. Do you know of any acts of kindness in Jake?"

"Jeff Nelsum once told of a time where Jake was walking down a sidewalk in Chicago and saw a man walking with a young girl of maybe eight years old. They were in conversation when suddenly the man bent down and slapped her hard across the face. Suddenly Jake ran up to the man and slammed him against a car holding him there, then suddenly let go and walked away."

"Thanks Jenna. It was good talking to you," said Rex, as he left just as quickly as he came.

As he walked out, he heard, "Thanks to you too. Come anytime."

Sheriff Hardy stopped at his office for an hour, then went home to sit and relax, mulling over actions coming his way if Jake came through, as he now hoped he would. It was now a time of patience waiting to see what Jake would be writing as he slept and rested to bring clarity to his thoughts.

Chapter Nineteen

April 29th seemed like a normal day in High Point, when Sheriff Hardy got the call early in the day from the nurse at the hospital. "Sheriff, the patient says he has written what he knows and is ready to meet."

Half an hour later both Chief Mathews and he were at the bed of Jake. He looked better than the day before, but a long way from feeling healthy. He never said a word, just handed the many pages he had written to Chief Mathews.

"Thank you Jake."

"Rest for a few minutes Jake. We want to scan what you have said. We will return," said the sheriff.

Jake had quite a story of how the trafficking worked and where, with some names recognizable. Most notable was the timing and locations. Both men soon came back to his bedside. Sheriff Hardy was quick to say, "I saw that courage and character the first day here. You won't regret this. That little girl on that Chicago sidewalk will be smiling today, remembering what you did for her when she got slapped so hard."

"How did you know about…" was all Jake could say as he looked at the men in disbelief.

Both men walked out of the hospital realizing how little time they had to prepare for what was to come. The first thing both men decided was how to use local law enforcement, to make sure federal authorities did not take all the credit, and try to run the entire thing, since the source of the information came from High Point law enforcement, in discovering this large network of child trafficking. They next shared that plan with Sheriff Briggs who agreed with how local law enforcement should be involved. They then made a conference call to the Federal Bureau of Investigation, explaining the involvement of local law enforcement and credit due them, before sharing crucial information. When the FBI realized the magnitude, they quickly agreed to meet within hours, to finish the planning. The time and place was set to be at a place that joins Iowa, Illinois and Wisconsin. The tactical part of it would be finalized at that meeting in privacy. The information gained from Jake established a pattern whereby captive children were taken across state lines, meaning the FBI would be present to intercept all those involved in one gigantic sweep. It would be a joint operation with a news conference at the end of it including key players. Photos of key known players on the criminal side of it would be shared by all law enforcement to make sure no one escaped.

Knowing that he only had a couple hours before the meeting, Sheriff Hardy had a few things he had to finish yet. He made a call to Harry Fixture, "Harry, I need your help for the next day or two. Can we meet at your antique shop now?"

"Yes. I am at your service, I assume as your deputy once again."

"That's right. I will be there in minutes," said Rex.

When they met, they did so with a hug, knowing there wasn't much these two wouldn't do for each other. "I want you to protect Jenna and Jim and Felicity for the next two days, if necessary. Be prepared for anything, and be careful not to be fooled by anyone. A big operation will be going on. I don't want to lose people I care about over payback or other such motives. Share this with these people in a limited way."

"When do you want me there?" asked Rex.

"One hour from now would help me feel better."

"I will be there. I thought this Chicago thing might get bigger. If you need me to come to you, call," said Harry, completely committed.

"I'll see you when I need you or when it is over. Thanks old friend."

Sheriff Hardy then left to make arrangements for someone to guard Jake's room at the hospital, just in case someone was interested in unfinished business. Sheriff Hardy now left for his meeting, knowing that following that meeting would come a flurry of activity, that he would try to disguise to the public. He approached his car and looked back over his city, wondering how often the FBI must look out the same way, wondering what future will be left, such a sobering thought.

Chapter Twenty

April 30th started with people finding their designated positions in High Point. Soon trucks would be coming from the north on their way to southern Wisconsin, Iowa and Illinois. Criminals were probably already positioned too. Law enforcement was aware of where they would be and made every effort to be non-visible until the order was given. Waiting was difficult. Timing was so important as to not let radio communication be completed in the transport of these young women.

At ten in the morning Sheriff Hardy got a call. "A truck is coming down highway 151 southward arriving in the High Point area about eleven."

The country road the old house was on had little traffic. With binoculars the sheriff's men and FBI agents could see a few men outside the house and in back, busily preparing for the truck. Each of the men had guns holstered and ready. They prepared for their assignment.

One of the men waved to the others, signaling sighting of the truck. No men were left outside as the truck drove into the driveway near the back door of the old house. The driver dressed in overalls and a black shirt stepped out of the truck. The passenger side man dressed in a red shirt, now did the same, and slowly walked to the back of the truck. An older man came out of the house now walking to the road, looking both ways. Seeing no vehicles he waved to them to proceed, which they did.

The man in the red shirt now opened the door at the back of the truck looking into the truck carefully, then waved to the house. Two men now walked out and motioned for the women to get up and step onto the ground in a line after being unchained from the inside wall. They did as they were told. When all twenty of them were out of the truck, one of the men stood behind them with his hand on his gun, and the other man led the women into the house. The older man from the road now walked back into the house. Only the truck remained.

An hour passed before any movement outside the house. The driver in the black shirt and the passenger in the red one stepped out behind the truck and opened the back door. Two of the women then were brought out and herded into the back of the truck and chained to the inside wall. The man with the red shirt locked the door, and both men took their previous positions in the front of the truck. The driver backed out onto the road and returned the way he came in on his way to highway 151 and was soon out of sight.

Five minutes later Sheriff Hardy's phone rang. "Another truck from the north has now passed highway 151 on its way to Iowa. When the truck from your High Point location reaches the next stop sign, our men will come out of hiding with guns pointed at the two men before they can warn anyone."

Fifteen minutes later the phone rang again. "The men were not expecting us at such a location. They have been taken into custody having made no calls. Two women are safe and being questioned now. Stay hidden unless someone tries to leave. Then call me."

An hour passed before the phone rang again. "The next truck has reached the position in Iowa as expected and is unloading their cargo of young women, fifteen women this time."

Sheriff Hardy suspected the same would happen there as did here. It was probably to feed the women and secure them. He found the waiting hard as he saw these women herded into places they would not want to go. He waited. An hour and fifteen minutes later, the phone rang. "Two men have driven away now. We will follow them to see if their part is finished, looking for the right moment to surprise them. Continue to wait."

Twenty minutes later the phone rang again. "The two men turned into a gas station to gas their vehicle. Our unmarked car pulled in giving our men a chance to make a purchase inside. One of the men in the truck on the passenger side left to visit a bathroom. One of our men waited for him to come out with a gun pointed at his head while the other tied a cloth tightly around his mouth to keep him quiet. He was then handcuffed and taken behind the gas station to wait for the driver. The driver went into the bathroom and came out to the same greeting. Both are now in custody. This time there were no women in the back of the truck. One other truck is seen coming down highway 151 presumably to Chicago. Wait if possible."

Sheriff Hardy knew it would take longer for that truck to get to Chicago. This is the part of the plan that worried him. Would some of the men at High Point choose this time to leave, thinking it was safe? It might call for creative action and luck to get them without them warning someone. He waited.

An hour had passed. Two men walked out of the house to smoke a cigarette looking down the road from which their truck had come. Were they waiting for someone to pick them up? Sheriff Hardy wondered. Both men then started walking down the road.

Sheriff Hardy then ordered his men. "Use the unmarked car and drive down the road and stop to offer these men a lift. If they accept, wait for them to get out, then step out and arrest them before they can reach their phones. If not, just drive on by and call me."

The men and the car drove out of sight leaving all to wait. Ten minutes or so later, the phone rang. "They accepted the ride and asked to get out at the stop sign to wait for a ride they said. When they started to walk away from us, we pulled our guns on them and quickly approached to get their phones and cuff them. They were not expecting it," said the deputy, pleased by the sound of his voice, as was Sheriff Hardy to hear how it went down.

Now the sheriff waited. A man came out of the house looking for the two men, then walked back in. No one came out again. The phone rang. "The truck got into Illinois but stopped at a country crossroad. We have all roads out of there blocked now expecting a shootout anytime, but will pull away quickly if it looks like the truck is on the road again. They must be suspicious. Any action on your end?"

Sheriff Hardy responded, "Two men left the house and walked down the road toward highway 151. I sent two undercover deputies to stop and see if they needed a ride. When they wanted out at the stop sign to wait for a ride, we arrested them without incident. Later a man came out of the house looking for them and went back in."

"That should not cause our guys to react the way they are. If shooting starts here, I will call and have you send in all your vehicles with loudspeakers asking them to give themselves up. Shoot as needed if it comes to that."

Fifteen minutes later came the call. "All is well again. It appears to be a bathroom stop in the country. They are on the road again coming back where they turned off. Continue to wait. It may be another hour."

It was more than an hour when the call came through. "While we waited for the truck to open doors, a car drove by speeding, causing the man in the front passenger side to start shooting at the car thinking they were caught. The car kept going. We will follow the same protocol. Wait."

An hour and fifteen minutes later the call came. "We arrested the truck drivers without incident. Now we are ready to use all the force we have as we go get the people in the house here. Do the same there at this time."

Sheriff Hardy gave the word. Law enforcement vehicles drove into the driveway in force while men walking came in from other angles. Over the loudspeaker could be heard, "Come out with your hands in the air. You are under arrest. Raids are occurring in Iowa and Illinois at this exact time. Come out with your hands in the air."

Lights went out as gunfire rang out from windows opening. Law enforcement did not return fire immediately unless able to see one of the men. With lights flashing on the house men could be seen firing.

Law enforcement fired back with screams now as some men were hit by bullets on both sides. A loudspeaker could be heard again. "This is the FBI. There will be no surrender if you keep shooting. Come out now or we come in."

There was a pause. Two men walked out, but not into the open, for fear their own men would shoot them. "We give up. We will move fast, but don't shoot."

Realizing the fear these cornered men might have, law enforcement saved all ammunition, in case shooting came from other parts of the house, from those who might want to shoot it out. It did not come until the two men had safely dived into the dark, where law enforcement took them aside in safety. Now two other men tried to run out the same door the first men did, but not with the purpose of giving up. They came out shooting blindly, with many law enforcement officers firing back, dropping them in their tracks.

After a quiet pause, a male voice could be heard, "We give up. We have had enough. We are outgunned. We will walk out with our hands raised."

They did just that and were taken into custody. Lights were turned on in the house as women now started filing out. There were only fifteen. Three were missing. Over the loudspeaker could be heard, "Anyone who can speak, please talk now."

"Help me," could be barely heard. Now law enforcement entered the building two at a time without being fired upon. They found the three women: one was shot in the leg, the other two were in the basement hiding in fear. Outside two officers were shot, one in the leg, and one in the arm as both men had protective gear on.

As the women were taken in vehicles to safety, the men inside who were shot, were brought out for medical care. Two were dead and one in serious condition. They obviously did not have protective gear. At this time Sheriff Hardy took the time to make a call to find out the fate of the others. At first there was no answer. Then came the call. "It is wrapped up in Iowa and Illinois. It started with gunfire at each place. Once they lost a couple men, they soon gave up and were arrested. A couple girls have been wounded, but will make it. The young women are being taken into safe places and questioned. The criminal suspects are being put in cells. In a while, let's talk to see if we have any of the leaders," said the FBI person in charge.

Chief Mathews now called, "I just wanted to check on our people. Did we lose any of them? As you know I was on the detail to follow the trucks and pick up the drivers and arrest them. It was a success here."

"A couple gunshot injuries, none serious. No one felt safe while it was going down though. Let's meet up at the sheriff's department where the prisoners are being taken to see if we can recognize anyone," said Sheriff Hardy.

He called Harry. "Harry, anything happening in High Point?"

"No. It is quiet here. We are all nervous. What can you tell me?"

"It was successful with injuries. Some suspects, who were not protected, were killed. The women are now safe. We are waiting to see if we recognize any of the suspects. Stay with your assignment. I can't be sure this is over yet, until we have the leaders locked up. I'll call when I can."

Chief Mathews and Sheriff Hardy met at the sheriff's department to take a look at the men jailed today, and booking information, to compare names to names given in Jake's notes. "Fred Cummlo, Bob Berlitze, Rich Knowlesko, and Jeff Nelsum are in jail here. Jerry Lensor was shot and died here," said the sheriff to Chief Mathews.

"It's getting late. Do you want to talk to them tomorrow morning?" asked Chief Mathews.

"Let me talk to FBI personnel first. I think it would be good if we could talk briefly with Rich Knowlesko yet tonight."

"Make the call," suggested the chief.

Sheriff Hardy made the call getting approval with one condition. FBI agent Cheryl Hanzli had to be present.

The three of them met Rich Knowlesko in a room set up for the interview. Cheryl Hanzli started the recording announcing all present in the room and the date of the interview. She started the interrogation with "Do you own the trucks transporting the young girls today?"

"I'm sure you already know that. Why ask?" said Rich.

"If I am insulting your intelligence, then give me the names of all involved in your criminal endeavors," she said mocking him.

"Again you insult me."

Sheriff Hardy intervened now. "Tell us something innocuous. Name patrons of Ted Donstayer's bar that you see from time to time."

"I don't see any harm in naming people I see socially. George Lafferole, Sue Deslin, Fred Cummlo, Jerry Lensor, David Ferind, and Bob Berlitze," said Rich, as if it was common knowledge and showing a bit of pompousness.

"Thank you for sharing what you know we already have. We are making progress now. Which of those people also go to the same nightclub you attend from time to time?"

"All of them at one time or another I suppose. There is no crime in being in a nightclub," stated Rich.

"Now give me names of women who attend both places."

"Is there a point to this?" asked Rich.

"I am trying to decide if you are being cooperative without causing harm," said the sheriff, hoping Rich would see him as a country boy not knowing any better.

"Sherry Halger, Sue Deslin, Jenna Boslin, Jane Chalmly, does that help you sheriff?"

"It does. How many of those have you personally seen this week?"

"That is more difficult to know since I am a busy person. If you mean which women, I can tell you Sherry and Sue. I have not seen George this week," answered Rich, assuringly.

"Where did you see Sherry?"

"I think it was at the club. She is there often enough," said Rich.

"One last question. Where and when did you see Sue today?"

"It must have been at Ted's bar earlier in the day," commented Rich.

FBI agent Cheryl Hanzli now asked, "Would you believe that we have known the whereabouts of all of these people today?"

"At some point in the day you may know such a thing. Most of us have few secrets," commented Rich, with a wise smirk.

"The question is how do you know such a thing?" she asked, trying to put him on the spot.

"Maybe I just like to think I do. I'm used to being a boss. It's a boss's prerogative." Rich said, being smug again.

"If it is any consolation, we do believe you are a boss in this child prostitution case," stated Cheryl, to see how strong his denial would be.

"I'm done answering your questions when you insult me. The next time you want to talk to me, I want my attorney present," was Rich's last statement.

The three of them left the room after turning off the recorder to meet in another room for a brief discussion. Rich was taken back to his cell.

In another room nearby Cheryl asked each of the men, "Did you learn anything from his glib answers that could help or hurt us?"

Chief Mathews had been listening carefully earlier. "How could he have known where Jenna Botlin was today? How come he did not mention Jake's name? Does he also know where he is today?"

"I checked on Jenna, but not on Jake at the hospital. It's late, but I'm going to call now, hoping they have not gotten their revenge for today. I would not put it past them," said Rex, feeling a sense of panic that maybe he wasn't as ready as he had thought.

He called the deputy he had left in charge of watching Jake, but got no answer. He called the hospital now asking for someone on the floor Jake was. A nurse finally answered. "What can I help you with sir?"

"This is Sheriff Hardy. I had a deputy guarding Jake. He does not answer. Would you go to the room to see if he or Jake is in there?"

"I will do it now."

She did not come back to the phone quickly. Then she screamed, "They are dead."

"Don't let anyone near the scene. I will send crime scene investigators now. Is that understood?"

"Yes I will prevent anyone from going near the room," she said crying.

Cheryl and the chief heard enough to act on it. Cheryl announced, "I will see to it that all routes out of the town where the hospital is are blocked. If the killer is still here, they either drove away or are still in town. We will also look for all out of state license plates in High Point. I will notify the Wisconsin State Patrol to look for suspicious driving behavior on highway 151 or excessive speeding."

The chief stated, "I will see that all cameras are viewed for activity today in High Point,"

Sheriff Hardy said, "I will notify crime scene people now. Before I go to the hospital myself, I must call the person guarding Jenna."

Harry Fixture answered immediately. "I'm still on the job. Should I be doing something different now, Rex?"

"I believe they know where Jenna is. The guard at the hospital and Jake have been murdered. Would you move your people to an even more secure room and lock all doors to the building, until I can get more help there."

"Will do."

The sheriff now ordered law enforcement vehicles to do drive-byes in the neighborhoods near the Best Bread and Breakfast.

Sheriff Hardy now drove to the hospital to see what could be learned about the assailant. He felt in his gut that the crime spree was not over. He had to somehow get ahead of it, but how? Who is this person, or is it more than one individual? How could they avoid being seen at the hospital? Should he work the scene or set a trap using Jenna as the bait? He could not help but think that the deed was done at the hospital. High Point has to be the target next, and it has to involve Jenna. The person or people involved have to be trying to clean up loose ends after the events of this day. They will be desperate, calling for desperate measures now, for law enforcement.

With no plan yet developed, Sheriff Hardy drove to the hospital looking for evidence that could lead him in the right direction. At the scene Sheriff Hardy met up with Cheryl Hanzli again, stepping up to her, saying, "You have anything, yet?"

"Not a lot. The deputy was shot in the back of the head, probably with a silencer on the gun. With blood on the floor, it appears he was dragged into the room where the killer then shot Jake, probably while he slept. I'm thinking the deputy, being tired, had just put his head down long enough for the killer to gain the advantage. Gloves were probably worn, as no prints have been found yet."

"Has anyone seen the killer coming or going?" asked the sheriff.

"It must have been close to dark, probably happening when all of us had our hands full at the three sites. It begs a question. Was the killer nearby finding out what was going down and came to clean up threats, or was the killer already here, not aware yet of problems in other places, and had previously planned this killing with great care?" mused Cheryl.

"I'm inclined to believe the plan was in the works prior to our sweep. I thought I had that possibility covered by planting guards over the two suspected victims. With one down I believe the other is at great risk. This killer may be smarter than I am. I'm leaning toward setting a trap verses waiting until we find this killer, especially since we don't even know if it is a man or a woman," was the worried thoughts of a weary sheriff.

"This could be the true leader of this operation. I'm in favor of bringing in the full force of the FBI to put an end to this threat. That kind of pressure could help this killer out of desperation to get careless."

"I agree that it is important enough and urgent enough to get all the help we can get. With that said, I more than ever feel the need to use Jenna as a target, while protecting her with everything we have," summed up all the emotions of Sheriff Hardy for Cheryl to see.

"Let's meet with a few of our best people to brainstorm how we can do this. I will call you when we can meet. You bring in Captain Mathews to the meeting also. Be in touch soon," said Cheryl firmly, as she walked out, leaving the sheriff hopeful again.

As the sheriff also walked out, a thought entered his mind. How is it we cannot find a car new to our area with all this police movement in this not so large community? The killer must have found a building not occupied. He would notify all law enforcement personnel of his thinking. One person had to know about this. He made the call. "I need your help in giving out buildings in our town not occupied to find where our killer could keep a vehicle hidden from view."

"I'm on it with the help of anyone I have left here, Rex," answered Chief Mathews.

"Great. I will also have you meet with the FBI in our attempt to plan how to draw out our killer."

The call came for a meeting at the local police station where local information was readily available. Cheryl and two FBI agents named Bill and Ted were there to meet with the chief and sheriff. The chief spoke first, "We have come up with several buildings where a vehicle could be hidden in our town with people visiting them. We will ask our people to be as careful as possible. If that doesn't work, we will think of houses or garages not in use."

"I know the night is passing us by. We have little time to plan: however, I wonder if we should let each of us know what suspects we have in custody to narrow down who this killer could be. In Iowa and Illinois we have the following in custody: Frank Kelzerole, David Ferind, Ted Donstayer, Franko Darenko, and Jack Ramset. Who of our possible suspects is left?" asked Cheryl of the group.

Five minutes passed before Chief Mathews said, "George Lafferole is the only one left of the men we know about. Should we be looking at women we know were involved?"

Bill said, "What choice do we have? Let's make a list of all of them left."

Sheriff Hardy started it, "Frieda Morsetty, Sue Deslin, Cindy Mcrobe, and Jane Chalmly. That is all I can come up with, some pretty unlikely."

Cheryl could only think of one or two remote possibilities, then said, "Bill, go now and call these people if need be to find out who is missing. Then call me and let me know. Use whatever resources you have to. Call me first about George Lafferole. It may be helpful to know it is only women killers we are after. Our files may be able to narrow it down."

"Now let's make our plan for early morning hours implementation. It starts in five minutes for whoever can be here," said Cheryl. That did not happen as Sheriff Hardy got a call. "A 911 call came in. There is gun fire at the Best Bed and Breakfast. Law enforcement vehicles are on their way and emergency vehicles."

Everyone left to make necessary arrangements, no one faster than the sheriff. He arrived at the scene with gun fire over, law enforcement there, as well as an ambulance. Sheriff Hardy rushed to the ambulance first. "Who has been shot?" he demanded, afraid of what he might hear or see.

A paramedic he recognized said, "Don't worry. We have it under control."

"Rex, I'm going to live. Relax," came the voice of Harry Fixture from inside the ambulance.

The paramedic then said, "He has been shot in the right shoulder. We are taking him to the hospital. Check on him there."

"Harry. Who shot you?" yelled the sheriff.

"It was a blond woman who was a good shot, but I hit her too," said Harry as the ambulance pulled away. Next, Rex ran to the building where it all happened, looking for Felicity, Jenna and Jim. Inside he found them all together talking with law enforcement. Felicity saw him coming and came running toward him, planting a hug and kiss on him, before either could speak, relief evident in each.

"Harry was heroic in protecting us, almost losing his own life. We will be just fine now. We are giving statements of what we saw and heard," Felicity said.

"Did you get a look at the shooter?"

"Not a good one, but Jenna thought she recognized something familiar in the brief view she had before getting down on the floor. She told me it might be someone she knew from the bar in Chicago, someone named Sue," said Felicity.

"Is that why they are talking to her now?"

"Yes and where to take her to keep her safe until this shooter is taken down," said Felicity.

By the time the sheriff could ask them, the decision had been made by the FBI agent. Seeing the sheriff walking toward him, the agent announced, "I think Jenna, Jim and Felicity should be taken to the sheriff's department for protection until we capture this woman shooter. Is there any problem with that?"

'I agree. Would you do that so that I can talk to Chief Mathews and focus on the area of our search?" said Sheriff Hardy.

"Will do that. We have shut down all roads out of High Point. Good luck," said the agent.

Sheriff Hardy called the chief. "I wondered how soon it would be before your call. I know what you want, so I will fill you in now. Everyone has been checking cars driving within ten blocks during the time of the shooting. A grey colored Toyota with Illinois license plates was seen driving toward highway 151, but there was no sign of the car there. She has gone into hiding within that ten block area."

"Would that be in an area of Jenna's home, the library, or the scene of the murder right after we learned of Jenna's problems?" asked Sheriff Hardy.

"It is. We are watching those areas. Meet me at Jenna's house now."

Moments later both men were there. The sheriff said, "We know Harry shot her, but not how bad the injury is. You cover the back while I cover the front. Be careful."

After a slow and careful look, they found nothing. There was only Jenna's car in the garage. Both men agreed to move on. Both were wondering where the car could be concealed. "We have not been to where Todd was killed for a while now. It's a long shot, but it is in the area. The family may have moved Todd's car by now, leaving an open garage," said the chief.

"You park in the back, and I will be in the front of the house. Take no chances and move carefully," said the sheriff.

"Let's approach from the side to see through the garage window what car is in the garage," suggested the chief.

"That is a good idea. Let's not be visible with our vehicles. We want to have the surprise if she is in the house," said the sheriff.

They arrived at the side of the garage with the sheriff's gun drawn, watching for her, while the chief peaked through the window. The chief nodded yes, with both men now taking positions on each corner of the garage to keep a view of back and front doors to prevent an escape. Then quiet calls were placed for backup including FBI. Both men knew it would be a short wait. They had to be ready in case she came out beforehand.

In minutes both men could see law enforcement people walking to secure the area before vehicles arrived in front of the house. There was still no sound from the house. A bullhorn sounded from the front, "This is the FBI. Open the front door and come out with your hands raised now."

Only quiet yet. A curtain moved ever so slightly from the front bedroom. It confirmed her presence. Over the speaker could be heard, "We know you are inside and wounded. Come out now without further bloodshed."

The front door opened. No one came out. Then a woman's voice. "I've been shot in the leg making it hard for me to move. I will throw my gun out. Don't shoot."

The screen door opened with her wearing a sweater, moving with a limp through the doorway and onto the grass. Law enforcement kept all guns on her, expecting resistance. She slowly raised her hands. Quickly, she lowered them, reaching for a gun at her waist, drawing and firing, before more shots rang out. All sound stopped as she fell just as quickly.

The FBI had anticipated suicide by police and were prepared as everyone was instructed to fire shots at her legs. Doing so forced her to drop so fast that the gun would come quickly out of her hand as she fell in pain. With her falling, men raced to the gun, as others raced to her with weapons drawn. Her plan did not succeed. The house was searched. Then she was taken in an ambulance to the nearest hospital.

The sheriff and police chief did not have to fire a shot. They were busy making sure no one else came running out. They were as certain as the lady that there would be no escape. The killing was over. Everyone on the scene felt a rush, not knowing how it would end. Many present felt tired from lack of sleep, welcoming a slower pace now in finishing this investigation. Sheriff Hardy looked at the face of this woman in pain, recognizing her as Sue Deslin. He wondered if she was the leader of the child trafficking, and how did she know about this house? Was she responsible for this murder? Sheriff Hardy knew it would soon come out, but right now all he wanted was some sleep, while others investigated the crime scene.

Chapter Twenty One

May 1st began with a tired police chief and sheriff being briefed by the FBI. Sue Deslin was in surgery after being shot several times in the legs. In her pants pocket was found a key to the house, suggesting she knew the place before today. As soon as others previously arrested knew of her capture, many were willing to testify for a shorter sentence, to her being the leader of the group. All feared her and said she had killed many.

Agent Cheryl Hanzli said, "A meeting with the press will be held at eleven this morning to announce that the community is safe again. A group of people will be said to be responsible for child trafficking in

Wisconsin, Iowa, and Illinois. Those accused of murder are now in the hands of law enforcement. More details will be forthcoming in the near future. A large thank you from the FBI will be given to law enforcement organizations in all three states, from police to sheriff departments, in helping to coordinate this investigation and make arrests."

Sheriff Hardy, confident that peace had now returned to his little part of the world, started to relax again. Still tired, he slowed his pace again to adjust to normalcy again in High Point. Rearranging his priorities again, first on his agenda was to visit his friends who had already been brought from the county jail to High Point. Knowing Felicity, he was sure she would want to be back in her Best Bed and Breakfast, and soon be ready for her customers again. With that in mind, Rex drove there to assess the damages and see his friends.

As he drove up, he could see some debris had been moved. Some areas were boarded up. A sign now said, "Open For Business." There was no doubt that Felicity was here.

He opened the door and walked in casually seeing the three of them eating a late breakfast. He slowly walked over, kissed Felicity on the cheek, saying, "Anything happening today. I'm a little bored with things being so quiet."

Felicity picked up a folded local newspaper and swatted him on the shoulder, saying, "Don't you act like everything is just fine. I don't ever want you to put me in such a position again," showing only a little bit of anger.

"I forgot to say. I'm so sorry about all the grief I have caused you three."

Jenna, Jim and Felicity all laughed. Jim spoke first. "I sure didn't know what I was getting into coming to High Point, Wisconsin."

Jenna looked at her brother saying, "You have been here when I needed you. I trust you won't let me down in the future." She then gave him a gentle hug.

"Wait just a minute, Jenna. Did I just hear you say the word trust? I didn't know you used that word often. Has there been a change?" said Rex.

"It took me some time to get there, didn't it? I have lived with fear for so long without confronting it. I didn't fully realize how much everyone needs to trust someone. The trick is knowing who and what to believe. My gut and my experiences are beginning to track that sort of thing in a more meaningful way now. Thanks," said an appreciative Jenna, putting her arms around Rex and Felicity now.

Rex now commented, "Jenna, you kept secrets to protect yourself for a long time. It not only didn't help you; it kept you discontent always. I have one last tip for you. The secret to happiness is to be content in any situation."

"Thanks Rex," responded a smiling, now happy, Jenna.

"I look forward to some more of these little chats in the future, but right now somebody has work to do." With that said, Rex walked slowly out to his vehicle and took a casual drive through his town. He knew it would take a few days to sort out all the details of life here in April of 2020.

Chapter Twenty Two

May 2nd was a quiet day with FBI personnel gone and no crimes of consequence reported in Iowa County for the sheriff. In fact he was looking forward to having guests at his home this evening. At seven the guests arrived, familiar ones: Felicity, Harry, Jim and Jenna.

As they sat down in the backyard in some lawn furniture, they relaxed and spoke freely. Jim said he had an announcement to make. "Tomorrow I will be leaving to go back to my home and start work again. I am fortunate to have an employer with patience and understanding. I will miss you, but I will return often."

Jenna spoke now saying, "I am announcing going back to work at the library tomorrow - full time again. I love what I do and can't wait to see my colleagues again."

Felicity said, "I am happy for both of you. Now Mr. Sheriff, I want to know more results of our crime wave. Share what you can."

"I finally got the story on Todd's murder. From confessions thus far, I discovered that Todd was supposed to be a part of helping the group bring young girls through our part of the state for a large sum of money. It seems he thought better of it and tried to back out. Sue paid him a visit one night and decided he would no longer be of use to her. Unsuspecting of such violence, Todd was unprepared and an easy target."

"She cleaned up afterward well. We are waiting for the fingerprint match from our early findings. Our community could not have foreseen any of it coming here," said Felicity.

"Jenna. Do you understand why people needed to kill you?" asked Rex.

"Obviously, I didn't for a long time. I heard them talking about taking women and didn't want to hear it, so I tried to put it out of mind forever and couldn't. I ran from it. You saw for yourself how that doesn't seem to work for most people, including me. With the help of people I trust, I hope I can make more informed decisions in the future," said a more confident young lady.

"Harry. Is your arm injury preventing you from talking tonight?" asked Rex.

"When have you known me to stay quiet? I am puzzled by Jake. He was the key to solving it all. It is unreasonable. How could you have known he was ready to make such a huge change in his life?"

"I've seen all kinds of people doing the worst of things on my job. Many in law enforcement get cynical by what they see too often. They lose their objectivity at times. Many young people especially don't have the ambition or will to get what they want the hard way, so they simply choose the easy way through life. As you know from experience, it doesn't work. It only leads to more trouble and less self-confidence, so they keep making the same mistakes feeling trapped in a life they don't want. That was the life of Jake."

"That's the part I understand, you silly man, you," expressed Harry in his usual humorous way.

"You must be referring to the change and how hard it is for people to deal with change. He got used to doing bad things and being paid well for it. He planned to continue that the rest of his life. He started seeing more people like Dick Rokpen who were desperate with someone trying to take advantage of their desperation. It riled him to the point he defended these people and found it gratifying. Then when he was asked to kill Jenna and failed, he recognized what he had become. He no longer wanted to be the one taking advantage, but rather the unexpected helper. Even though he was a killer, he no longer wanted to be remembered for that. Being captured for his attempt on Jenna's life hurt his confidence. When the chief and I interrogated him with gentle kindness about good people in his life, he folded. He gave up all he knew to help us release him from his world of desperation no matter what the outcome. He became a free man."

"That is such a sad story," said Jenna with tears in her eyes.

"Not at all. It is a story of redemption. It is a joyous story that few will ever know," shouted Felicity.

"It's the kind of story the history books won't tell even if they find out years later," said Jim.

"That's cynical, brother of mine," said Jenna, seriously now.

"I have the solution then. We will make it a Netflix original movie," snapped back the witty Harry Fixture.

"I don't think there will be a memorial service held for Jake. Why do you think people go to memorial services?" asked Rex.

"I suspect there isn't much in his life that is memorable?" said Jim.

"What do you expect to hear when you attend a memorial service?" asked Harry of Rex.

"If you don't mind, I will start earlier than death. How do we form our beliefs and when? Most of it starts with early memories of childhood with parents, grandparents, maybe churches, and people read about or well known. For too many people those beliefs stay the same til death. It's a little different for those we hear about in memorials. For these people, the beliefs change throughout life, as experiences change. All have bad things happen to them; however, some of us have the good fortune to have good people there to help us through it all. As we grow through those experiences, we appreciate them more and start behaving differently than previously. The good of the good people rubs off! It helps us have more faith and trust in others. When the good die, there are many there to send them on their way, respectfully, in appreciation for all they have done for them and others."

Harry responded too quickly, "You sit there hearing others talk about all this person did. It can get tiring. No one is perfect, not even the good."

"You are missing the point my friend. It isn't about being perfect. It is about being all you can be for yourself and others, that separates you from so many. It is what you do that counts in life, not just your mistakes. People don't show up to hear about all your mistakes. Anyone can make mistakes. Doing something worthwhile with your life is satisfying beyond words," was Rex's last statement on the subject. Later that night he went to sleep thinking about his father.

The next morning Rex woke up again with his father on his mind. He remembered a time when young, riding with his father on the path across the state of New York early one morning, driving east into the sun. It left such an impression on his young mind seeing that sun rise so brightly, making it hard to see to drive. It made the earth look flat, as that sun kept rising over that sharp earth's edge into the sky in such beauty. It was a wonder to grab hold of.

The next day he remembered walking up a steep incline in Massachusetts to get a better view of the mountains. When he and his father finally reached the top, both looked out over a blue sky as pure and clear as any ever seen. He was so involved in that sight that he failed to see an old man and a young girl sitting with their backs to him, on a bench called Poet's Seat, looking out at the same sky with renewed hope together.

Now on this day in High Point, Rex thought of that scene in a new light. He saw himself in the old man valuing the experiences of life, but he thought even more about the young girl, so innocent, full of joy, experiencing the moment in all its fullness. He found himself hoping she would value her experience in differentiating good and bad in people she would meet, to make wise decisions in knowing who to trust, showing her the good, and the direction to it.

Rex then realized it applies to people of all ages. We must strive to keep our integrity to maintain and grow ourselves forward.

Made in the USA
Middletown, DE
25 May 2021